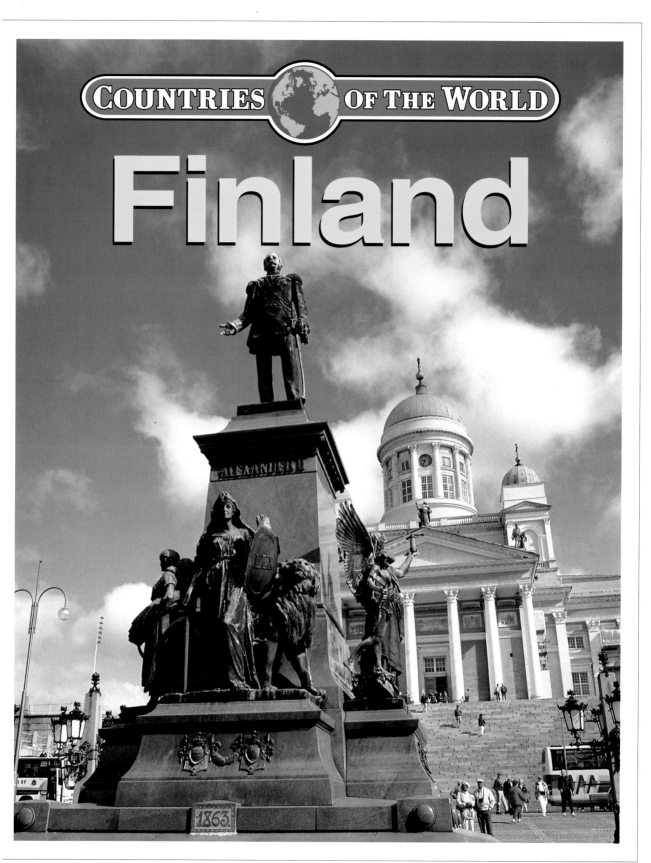

COUNTRIES OF THE WORLD

Finland

Gareth Stevens Publishing
A WORLD ALMANAC EDUCATION GROUP COMPANY

About the Author: Zhong Meichun lives and works in Singapore. She studied journalism and has written for local newspapers and magazines.

Written by
ZHONG MEICHUN

Edited by
JUNIA BAKER

Designed by
LYNN CHIN

Picture research by
SUSAN JANE MANUEL

First published in North America in 2001 by
Gareth Stevens Publishing
A World Almanac Education Group Company
330 West Olive Street, Suite 100
Milwaukee, Wisconsin 53212 USA

For a free color catalog describing
Gareth Stevens' list of high-quality books
and multimedia programs, call
1-800-542-2595 (USA) or
1-800-461-9120 (CANADA).
Gareth Stevens Publishing's
Fax: (414) 332-3567.

© **TIMES MEDIA PRIVATE LIMITED 2001**
Originated and designed by
Times Editions
An imprint of Times Media Private Limited
A member of the Times Publishing Group
Times Centre, 1 New Industrial Road
Singapore 536196
http://www.timesone.com.sg/te

Library of Congress Cataloging-in-Publication Data
Zhong, Meichun.
Finland / by Zhong Meichun.
p. cm. -- (Countries of the world)
Includes bibliographical references and index.
ISBN 0-8368-2331-1 (lib. bdg.)
1. Finland--Description and travel--Juvenile literature. [1. Finland.]
I. Title. II. Series.
DL1015.4 .M45   2001
948.97--dc21   00-056349

Printed in Malaysia

1 2 3 4 5 6 7 8 9 05 04 03 02 01

Contents

5 AN OVERVIEW OF FINLAND

6 Geography
10 History
16 Government and the Economy
20 People and Lifestyle
28 Language and Literature
30 Arts
34 Leisure and Festivals
40 Food

43 A CLOSER LOOK AT FINLAND

44 Architecture
46 Communications Superpower
48 Etiquette
50 Finnish Sauna: A National Tradition
52 Fishing and Water Sports
54 Land of the Midnight Sun
56 Medieval Castles
58 Midsummer Bonfires
60 Modern Design
62 Money Grows on Trees
64 Protecting the Forests
66 Sami, the Native People of Finland
68 Santa Claus
70 Seafood Galore
72 Women in Finland

75 RELATIONS WITH NORTH AMERICA

For More Information …
86 Full-color map
88 Black-and-white reproducible map
90 Finland at a Glance
92 Glossary
94 Books, Videos, Web Sites
95 Index

AN OVERVIEW OF FINLAND

A land of extraordinary natural beauty, Finland, or *Suomi* (SOR-mee), is often described as "the country of thousands of lakes." More than 187,000 lakes are surrounded by dense forests of spruce and pine. In winter, snow covers the trees, and lakes are frozen, but in summer, Finland is a paradise for nature lovers.

Finland is a northern European area settled originally by tribes from Russia. The Swedes, however, occupied Finland for hundreds of years, and Swedish influence is still evident in the historical and cultural ties between Finland and Sweden.

Finland is one of the most technologically advanced countries in Europe. Its manufacturing sector focuses on engineering, electronics, and telecommunications.

Opposite: **Finns love to fish, both in summer and winter. One out of every three Finns fishes for recreation.**

Below: **Finnish children gear up for backpacking in a nature reserve.**

THE FLAG OF FINLAND

The Finnish flag is white with an ultramarine-blue Nordic cross that stretches to the edges of the flag. One poet has said that the two colors represent the blue of the lakes and the white snow of winter. The national flag is unadorned, but the state flag, which is flown on government buildings, has the Finnish coat of arms in the center. The crest is a gold lion bearing a sword and standing on a curved Russian saber. The lion is surrounded by nine white roses, all on a red background. The flag of Finland was adopted in 1919, two years after the nation gained independence from Russia.

Geography

Finland is the fifth largest country in Europe, with a total area of 130,128 square miles (337,032 square kilometers). It is a long, narrow country sandwiched between the Russian Federation to the east and Sweden to the west. Norway lies to the north, while the southern and southwestern coasts stretch 683 miles (1,099 km) along the Gulfs of Finland and Bothnia.

The southern and western coastal areas are less densely forested than most of the country, with low plains and rich soil fed by the many rivers that flow through the country and into the Gulf of Bothnia. The majority of the population lives in this area, where the relatively mild climate is pleasant and the fertile soil is good for farming.

Over 30,000 scenic islands dot the southern and western coastlines. Some of the islands are barren rock, while others teem with plant and animal life. The biggest island chain is the Åland archipelago, with 6,500 islands situated halfway between Finland and Sweden.

LAND OF THE MIDNIGHT SUN

In northern Finland, the sun does not set for two months in summer. Even in the south, daylight lasts twenty hours. In winter, two months of darkness are lit by nature's light show, the aurora borealis.
(A Closer Look, page 54)

Below: **The Åland archipelago has thousands of islands. Some are sparsely populated, while others are summer playgrounds for visitors and tourists.**

Forests and Lakes

Finland's two most abundant natural resources are its forests and lakes. About 76 percent of the country is covered by forests. The trees are mainly pine and spruce, but some birch, aspen, and alder trees grow here as well. In the southwest, oak, linden, elm, and ash trees thrive.

Inland water covers about 10 percent of Finland's area, with lakes, ponds, rivers, creeks, and rapids. Small lakes join with shallow rivers and canals to form large lake systems and natural waterways. Finland's largest lake, Saimaa, has more than one hundred interconnected smaller lakes, with a total area of 443 square miles (1,147 square km).

Almost one-third of the country lies north of the Arctic Circle. The northernmost province, called Lapland, has the harshest climate and the least-fertile soil in the country. The country's forests are sparse here, and vegetation on hills and marshland is stunted. In the far north, the land becomes a flat, treeless plain. Only in the northwest is the terrain broken by mountains. The highest mountain is Haltiatunturi at 4,344 feet (1,324 m).

Above: **In autumn, the leaves on birch trees turn yellow, while pine and spruce trees remain green.**

FINLAND'S THREE LEGS

Because Finland's largest exports were once metal and wood, it was said that the country had two "legs." Now it has three legs; in 1998, electronics exports surpassed the exports of both wood and metal.

Seasons

Finland has a cold climate with four seasons. The longest season is winter, when temperatures may drop as low as -22° Fahrenheit (-30° Celsius) in the north and -4° F (-20° C) in the south. Yet Finnish winters are still somewhat warmer than winters in other countries at similar latitudes because of a warm ocean current that flows off the Norwegian Sea. Temperatures in the north average -8° F (-22° C) in winter, while in summer they may rise as high as 80° F (27° C). Farther south, temperatures are somewhat less extreme, ranging from 22° F (-6° C) in winter to 72° F (22° C) in summer.

In the far northern part of Finland, the sun does not set for two months in the height of summer. In winter, the sun remains below the horizon for almost two months. This polar night is called *Kaamos* (KAH-mohs). Snow arrives as early as October and lasts through April. On north-facing mountains, the snow remains all year long. Even in the far south on the Åland Islands, snow covers the ground for about ninety days each year.

Above: Skis and snowmen are common sights in Finland, even in April.

ARCTIC CIRCLE

The Arctic Circle is a line of latitude around Earth that marks the area most affected by the midnight sun. Places north of this line usually experience one day in June with no night and one day in December with no daylight. The number of continuous days in the summer and continuous nights in winter gradually increase, moving northward toward the North Pole.

Plants and Animals

Coniferous forests are found all over Finland. The two main types of trees here are pine and spruce. Roaming the many forests are wild animals, such as elks, foxes, lynxes, hedgehogs, wolverines, and wolves. In northern regions, reindeer wander freely. The largest animal in Finland is the brown bear, which was once so feared that even mentioning its name was taboo. Only several hundred bears remain, and they are protected by law. Elks, however, are hunted legally every year because they are numerous and often cause severe road accidents.

Over three hundred species of birds live in Finland, including the black grouse, whooper swan, and birds of prey, such as the osprey and eagle. Chaffinches and willow warblers are commonly found in the forests, while sparrows tend to appear in inhabited areas. Over seventy species of fish, such as Baltic herring, whitefish, and salmon, are in the many lakes. The most commercially important saltwater fish is the Atlantic herring.

Above: **Thistles are wildflowers that grow everywhere in Finland. They are usually pink and have prickly leaves.**

Left: **Wolverines, members of the weasel family, live in cold, northern latitudes, especially heavily timbered areas. They look like small bears but smell like skunks.**

MONEY GROWS ON TREES

The forests and farms of Finland were once great sources of income. Before 1950, most Finns farmed in summer and worked in timber-related businesses in winter. Today, only about 7 percent of the Finnish workforce is involved in agriculture.

(A Closer Look, page 62)

History

The first trace of human settlement in Finland dates back to the end of the last Ice Age some 10,000 years ago. Imprints of wandering hunters and nomads were found in rock paintings from the Stone Age (7500–1500 B.C.).

The Finno-Ugric peoples, from what is now central Russia, were part of the earliest known migrations, or movements of peoples from one place to another. Later, the Tavastians and Häme came from southwestern Europe and the Karelians from central Europe. These early ancestors of the Finns were spread across southern Finland and did not join together to form one nation or create a central government. The country was an easy target for control by other nations, particularly by its immediate neighbors, the Catholic Swedish empire to the west and Eastern Orthodox Russia to the east. The Swedish gradually established control over the area during the twelfth century.

MEDIEVAL CASTLES

When Finland was under Swedish control, many castles were built to defend the country. Today, these castles are museums, government centers, and sites for performing arts.
(A Closer Look, page 56)

Below: Turku was the capital of Finland until 1808. Turku Castle protected the citizens from invasions for centuries after it was built in 1280.

Left: Eighteenth-century cannons are displayed at Suomenlinna Fortress. The fortress is on five interconnected islands and was built to guard the sea approach to Helsinki.

SAMI, THE NATIVE PEOPLE OF FINLAND

The Sami (SAH-mee) were among the earliest settlers of Finland. They still live in Lapland and have preserved many of their traditions.

(A Closer Look, page 66)

Pre-Independence

The first Christian missionaries from Sweden arrived in Finland in 1155. Together with the Swedish immigrants who followed, these missionaries firmly planted the roots of Christianity in the southwestern region. Meanwhile, Russia — known as Novgorod at the time — spread its influence along the Gulf of Finland. These two countries were to compete for control of Finland for the next six hundred years.

Finland became part of the Swedish realm in 1323, when the Swedes and Russians signed the Treaty of Nöteborg to mark political boundaries. Sweden gained control over most of present-day Finland, except for the eastern territory of Karelia, which became part of Russia. Sweden had significant influence on the development of Finnish political, economic, and social life, especially in developing a central government and granting the Finns self-rule and equal rights with Swedes.

Despite the Treaty of Nöteborg, between 1500 and 1790, Russia and Sweden continued to fight over control of Finland, and, in 1809, Russia took possession. Russia allowed Finland to have its own government and other freedoms.

Below: King Gustave III (1746–1792), a Swedish king who also ruled Finland, was known for his enlightened reforms. He encouraged free trade between nations and was a champion of freedom of the press. A monument to him is shown below.

An Independent Country

In the beginning, Russia respected Finland's independent status. Finns began to speak Finnish, instead of Swedish, and take pride in their heritage. They adopted a modern parliamentary form of government, in which all people were equally represented, and had their own army.

In the 1890s, however, Russia took away many of these freedoms. Finns could no longer make their own laws, and the army was dissolved. The people resisted fiercely and formed a Finnish liberation movement, but they never actually had to declare war. The revolution and downfall of the Russian monarchy in 1917 freed Finland from Russian rule. On December 6, 1917, Finland proclaimed its independence. Two years later, the constitution and national flag were adopted, and Finland became a democratic republic headed by a president.

As World War II approached, Finland tried to remain neutral but was drawn into the conflict when the Soviet Union invaded in

Above: Torches commemorate Finnish independence from Russia, which was gained on December 6, 1917. The statue silhouetted against the sky is of Carl Gustaf Emil Mannerheim, hero of the Winter War and former marshal of Finland.

1939. The war with the Soviets, called the Winter War, lasted only a few months, and Finland lost despite fierce resistance. In 1941, Finland allowed the Germans to station troops in the country, and Germany invaded the Soviet Union from the Finnish border. In retaliation, the Soviet Union bombed Finland, and this time the two countries were at war until 1944. In the negotiated peace, Finland had to give up part of the province of Karelia and pay heavy reparations to Russia.

After the war, Finland set about rebuilding the nation. The country had been badly damaged by the wars with the Soviet Union and by the Germans, who had destroyed villages and burned forests as they retreated from Finland. In 1948, Finland signed the Treaty of Friendship, Cooperation, and Mutual Assistance with the Soviet Union, agreeing to prevent any attack on the Soviet Union from Finnish territory.

In the years that followed, Finland was burdened by heavy debt in the form of war reparations to the Soviet Union. There were also many refugees from Soviet Karelia who needed homes and employment. Finland reorganized its industrial infrastructure and focused on engineering and manufacturing. By 1952, the war reparations were paid in full, and Finland had friendly relations with the Soviet Union.

COMMUNICATIONS SUPERPOWER

The often-taciturn Finns love to communicate when it comes to telephones and the Internet. More than half the population owns mobile telephones, and one in every ten Finns uses the Internet.
(A Closer Look, page 46)

Left: **Finnish soldiers fought on skis during the 1939 Winter War with the Soviet Union.**

Modern Finland

In 1955, Finland joined the United Nations. The following year, Urho Kekkonen became president. He pursued a foreign policy known as the "Paasikivi-Kekkonen line" and kept Finland out of conflicts with other nations with skillful diplomacy. Finland has remained a neutral country, maintaining good relations and trade agreements with all nations, especially the Scandinavian countries and the Soviet Union, now the Russian Federation.

In the early 1970s, Finland hosted the Strategic Arms Limitation Talks between the Soviet Union and the United States. A few years later, thirty-five nations met in Helsinki for the Conference on Security and Cooperation in Europe (CSCE). Finland currently works with United Nations peacekeeping forces in developing nations, such as Bosnia and Lebanon.

Finland suffered a period of economic decline after the collapse of the Soviet Union in the late 1980s, partly because the Soviet Union had been its main trading partner. By 1995, however, its economy was again prosperous. Finland joined the European Union on January 1, 1995.

Below: **President Urho Kekkonen addresses participants of the CSCE Summit, held at Finlandia Hall, Helsinki, in July 1975.**

Elias Lönnrot (1802–1884)

Elias Lönnrot, a literature professor, was the compiler of the *Kalevala*, or *Land of Heroes*, Finland's national folk epic. This collection of folk songs and poems, in the Finnish language, is the foundation of Finnish culture. Published in 1835, the *Kalevala* inspired many artists and composers.

Elias Lönnrot

Minna Canth (1844–1897)

Finnish playwright Minna Canth was a feminist who had a powerful impact on nineteenth-century Finland. Her works explored the status of women and workers in Finnish society. Her literary career began in 1878 with short stories, followed by a book in 1879 and her first play in 1880. As a widow, she raised seven children while managing a family-owned shop. Her most famous play, *The Pastor's Family*, was about social conditions and crises in a middle-class family.

Carl Gustaf Emil Mannerheim (1867–1951)

Carl Gustaf Emil Mannerheim, the greatest general in Finnish history, was a hero of the Winter War against the Soviet Union. His military career started in 1882, when he enlisted in the Russian army; he later fought in the Russo-Japanese War (1904–1905). When Finland declared its independence, Mannerheim was named commander-in-chief of the Finnish armed forces. He raised an army from scratch and trained the soldiers to fight. After the two wars with the Soviet Union, he became president of Finland. He served for two years before he retired in 1946 because of ill health.

Carl Mannerheim

Paavo Nurmi (1897–1973)

Paavo Nurmi was known as the Flying Finn. He was the best-known long-distance runner in Finland, winning a total of nine gold and three silver medals in the Olympics in the 1920s. His achievements introduced Finland, then a young, independent country, to the rest of the world. Nurmi set a total of twenty-five world records in his twelve-year career. He was regarded as Finland's unofficial ambassador of goodwill.

Paavo Nurmi

Government
and the Economy

Government

Since its independence in 1917, Finland has been a democratic republic. The Finnish constitution, adopted in 1919, gives all citizens extensive individual rights. Anyone over eighteen years of age may vote.

The head of state is the president, who is elected by the people every six years. The president has supreme executive power, is in charge of the country's foreign policy, and has the right to endorse or reject bills in the parliament. In February 2000, Tarja Halonen was elected Finland's first female president.

The parliament elected in March 1999 is made up of 200 members from seven different political parties. Members are elected by popular vote to four-year terms. Over one-third of the members are women. The parliament is headed by the prime minister. The current prime minister is Paavo Lipponen.

Below: The Finnish Parliament building is in Helsinki. Leading political parties include the Social Democratic Party, the Center Party, the National Coalition (Conservative) Party, the Swedish People's Party, the Leftist Alliance, the Green Union, and the Finnish Christian League.

Judicial power lies in the independent courts of justice. The justices of high courts are appointed by the president. Since 1919, Finland has had an ombudsman, an impartial officer who oversees and investigates complaints by individuals against actions of the government.

Above: **Porvoo, a short distance northeast of Helsinki, still looks like a nineteenth-century small town. When Finland was a part of Russia, the first Finnish government met in Porvoo's Town Hall.**

Provinces and Municipalities

Finland is divided into six provinces and 455 municipalities, or local authorities. The provinces are headed by provincial governors who are appointed by the president and are directly responsible to the central government. Each municipality is headed by an elected council, which determines the municipal tax rate and is in charge of urban planning and provision of services, such as water supply, electricity, and sewerage.

The municipalities receive funds from the government to provide welfare services, such as child care, health care and hospitalization, basic education, and firefighting and rescue services. They also maintain a system of local libraries that is considered one of the most extensive in the world.

Above: **Factories line the waterfront in Tampere, a major industrial city in the lake region.**

Economy

Finland was traditionally an agricultural country, but today only 8 percent of the land is cultivated. The farms produce hay, potatoes, oats, and barley, as well as dairy products, meat, poultry, and eggs. In recent years, Finland has made a swift transition to a highly industrialized and urbanized country. Today, the Finnish economy is made up mainly of forest products, engineering, and electronics.

Forests are Finland's most important natural resource. Pulp, paper, and timber account for about 40 percent of Finland's exports. Mineral deposits, such as copper, iron ore, and zinc, are found in Finland's bedrock and are extracted for domestic use. Finland is a world leader in mining technology, ore processing, and metallurgy.

With industrialization, the metal and engineering industries, as well as wood processing, have developed rapidly. Today, these industries are the largest sources of urban employment. They also

MODERN DESIGN

For centuries, glassworks factories have produced practical but beautiful items for the home. Finnish designers make everything from classic vases to enamel pots.

(A Closer Look, page 60)

produce the country's main exports. Finland also manufactures machinery for the timber and wood processing industries, such as paper machines and forest tractors.

Electronics was the fastest growing industry in Finland in the 1990s. Nokia is Finland's flagship company in electronics and telecommunications. Kone, a Finnish elevator manufacturer, is the world's third-largest producer of elevators.

The chemical, graphics, food, textile, and electrochemical industries are also important to the Finnish economy. The chemical industry is dominated by Kemira, which produces fertilizers and paints, and Neste, which refines oil, distributes natural gas, and specializes in international trade and marketing.

Foreign Trade

Finland's five biggest trading partners are Germany, Sweden, the United Kingdom, the United States, and the Russian Federation. Major exports are electrical and telecommunications equipment and pulp and paper. Other exports include machinery, metals, chemicals, and transportation equipment. Finland is self-sufficient in agricultural goods but imports many other items, including raw materials, mineral fuels, and consumer goods.

Below: **Many Finnish factories produce beautiful household goods, such as highly glazed and colorful enamel cookware.**

People and Lifestyle

Who Lives in Finland?

Just over five million people live in Finland, making it the third least-populated country in Europe. Nearly 98 percent of all people living in Finland were born in the country. Many Finns have blond hair, fair skin, and blue eyes. The typical Finn has inherited 75 percent Swedish or other Scandinavian blood and 25 percent from Finland's indigenous peoples.

The main ethnic minority groups are the Sami of Lapland and the Romany. The Sami were part of the earliest migrations of Finno-Ugric peoples from the east 6,000 years ago. Today, some 5,700 live in Lapland, the northernmost part of Finland. About 6,000 Romany people also live in Finland and are distributed evenly throughout the country. Finland has one of the lowest proportions of foreigners in Europe; they make up only about 1 percent of the population.

FINNISH SAUNA: A NATIONAL TRADITION

Saunas are steam baths created by throwing water on heated stones. The Finns believe that a sauna cleanses the body and rejuvenates the soul. (*A Closer Look, page 50*)

Below: Many Finns are Nordic, a term that defines a person from northern Europe. It also refers to people who have fair hair and skin and light eyes.

The Finnish Character

The Finns are known for their honesty and strength of character. The Finnish word *sisu* (SEE-soo) defines their ideal personality — strong, independent, and courageous. A person possessing these qualities will strive to conquer adversity with stamina, courage, and sometimes obstinacy.

Finns also value privacy. Their summer homes are often in remote locations. They tend to speak quietly and are surprised when people talk loudly. They do not typically show affection in public, and shaking hands is more common than kissing cheeks.

Finnish Homes

Finnish housing is of high quality. About 75 percent of all Finns live in towns, and over half of them live in Helsinki, Turku, and Tampere. The typical Finnish home is a single-family house or apartment. More than 60 percent of all Finns own their homes, while 20 percent live in government-provided housing, and 20 percent rent their homes. Many Finns also own second homes in rural areas. There are nearly 400,000 summer cottages in southern Finland, both along the coast and in the eastern lake areas.

Above: **Finnish summer cottages are often nestled in the forest near one of the country's many lakes.**

ETIQUETTE

Bowing is a sign of respect in Finland. People tend to shake hands, even when they meet a good friend. They also take spoken agreements very seriously, so visitors need to think twice before making verbal agreements.
(A Closer Look, page 48)

21

Family Life

The average Finnish family has 3.7 members, or less than two children per family. Usually both the husband and wife work, and they share family decisions and burdens. The wife, with some help from the husband, usually does the housework, prepares breakfast, and takes the children to school. On weekends, the family spends time together, mostly in the outdoors. During the summer, many families spend weekends at their summer homes by the lakes or on the coast.

Most Finns are married in churches, often in spring or summer. Usually, the bride's family hosts a dinner reception, at which the bride and groom cut their wedding cake, dance, and receive gifts from the guests. Today, wedding costs are often shared by the parents of both the bride and the groom.

Since families are small in Finland, a newborn receives a lot of attention. Friends crowd the house, bringing food, clothes, and gifts to celebrate the birth of a child. Finland's infant mortality rate — less than four deaths in every thousand births — is one of the lowest in the world.

Above: **Many Finnish married couples have only one or two children.**

Roles of Men and Women

Finland's men and women enjoy equal status and are equally well-educated. They both have had the right to vote since 1906. They each make up 50 percent of the Finnish student population and workforce, and they both have the right to volunteer for national service.

Finnish women are proud of what they have achieved. They lead very independent lives, and most continue working after marriage. About 70 percent of all Finnish women work outside the home, and they value their own individual needs, training, and careers.

The government supports this independence with legislation that calls for equal rights for women in the workplace. Legislation also ensures that employers provide 258 days of paid maternity leave and three subsequent years of unpaid leave.

In the rural areas of Finland, however, work is still defined by gender. Men work in the fields and operate machinery. Women tend the livestock, cook, care for the children, and clean both the house and barn.

WOMEN IN FINLAND

Since they entered the legislature in 1907, Finnish women in parliament have had a significant impact on the growth and direction of their government. The country's first female president, Tarja Halonen, was elected in 2000.

(A Closer Look, page 72)

Below: Chic businesswomen shop over their lunch break.

Education

Education is free in Finland. All children between the ages of seven and sixteen receive compulsory education in comprehensive schools. Parents may place their children in either a Finnish-language or Swedish-language school. After comprehensive school, students may leave school or choose to attend a high school for three years or a vocational school for two to five years.

The Finnish educational system emphasizes foreign languages, especially English, Russian, French, and German. Children study three foreign languages before they even enter high school.

After high school, students may choose to attend college, a polytechnic school, or a vocational school. Finland has more than twenty universities and institutes, with a total student population of 130,865, of whom 52 percent are women. Some students go on to earn doctorates. Universities are owned by the state, and most students receive state grants and subsidized health care. At vocational schools, students are trained in auto mechanics, hairdressing, and other trade skills.

Below: **Pupils — and teacher — study in a Helsinki elementary school. Children attend school from 8:00 a.m. to 2:00 p.m. Lunch is free, and some schools offer breakfast as well.**

The Mark of Adulthood

White caps and red roses traditionally mark a Finnish teenager's transition to adult life. Some leave school at the age of sixteen, after completing the compulsory nine years of school. Those who stay on, however, until they are eighteen and pass the comprehensive examination for entrance to a university, are entitled to the traditional ceremony.

Each year, on the last Saturday of May, high school students assemble in their school halls to receive their examination certificates. All the graduates wear white caps, and the girls carry red roses. They return home to celebrate their graduation with friends and relatives.

Above: **Graduates from the Class of 1996 at Itakeskus High School in Helsinki wear white caps.**

The Reading Habit

Finns are avid readers, and Finland's literacy rate is 100 percent. Finns buy books from the country's many bookstores or borrow them from one of the 1,500 public libraries. Each Finn borrows an average of eighteen books a year. Besides novels, Finns read magazines, classical literature, and academic works.

Religion

Christianity first came to Finland in the twelfth century. It was spread by Catholic missionaries from Sweden, but Catholicism did not make a lasting impression on the country. In the sixteenth century, Finns embraced the Lutheran faith instead.

Above: **Tampere Cathedral was designed by Lars Sonck in 1907.**

Mikael Agricola (1510–1557), who is credited with founding the written Finnish language, became the first bishop of Turku in 1554. Lutheranism was declared the official religion of the country in 1593, and today, almost all Finns are Lutheran.

During the nineteenth century, when Finland was an autonomous state under Russia, the Eastern Orthodox Church flourished in the country. Today, it is the second largest church in Finland, with a following of 54,000 worshipers.

A small portion (about 1 percent) of the population belongs to other faiths, including Jehovah's Witnesses, Adventists, Catholics, and Jews, while another 9 percent are not affiliated with any religious organization.

The relationship between the Lutheran Church and the state was defined by church law in 1869. The state supports the church financially, and church laws cannot be made without the approval of the president and parliament. Bishops are appointed by the president, with advice from the church.

Freedom to Worship

In 1922, the Finns were granted complete freedom of religion. A citizen may legally withdraw from the national church and belong to another church or no church at all. Parents today also may decide whether their children study religion in school.

The Evangelical Lutheran Church of Finland has 600 parishes and 4.4 million followers. Finns of all age groups attend church ceremonies, including baptisms, confirmations, marriages, and funerals, but many do not attend church on a regular basis.

Both the Lutheran and Eastern Orthodox churches receive financial assistance from the state. The funds are used for educational and social service programs. Churches help the aged and disabled, alcoholics, drug addicts, and low-income families; run family counseling centers; and organize self-help activities for the unemployed. Some 19,000 people are employed by churches, including social workers, child-care workers, and musicians.

Above: **Lumi Lina Snow Castle in Kemi is built every winter and includes a chapel.**

NAME DAYS

Celebrating a person's name day is a long-standing tradition in Finland. Most days of the year are associated with certain names, often those of saints, such as St. Stephen's Day. Finns celebrate both their name days and their birthdays.

Left: Built in 1868, Uspenski Cathedral in Helsinki is Europe's largest Eastern Orthodox Church.

Language and Literature

Finland has two official languages: Finnish and Swedish. Finnish is spoken by about 94 percent of the population, and about 6 percent speak Swedish. Unlike other European or Scandinavian languages, Finnish is a Finno-Ugric language and is similar to Estonian and Hungarian. Finnish is difficult for foreigners to learn because the same word is used for "he" and "she," and the language has few articles, such as "a" and "the." The interchangeable word order of subject, verb, and object is also confusing to a foreigner.

Finnish literature dates back to the sixteenth century. Mikael Agricola was the first person to put the language in writing. He wrote the first Finnish alphabet, then translated the New

Below: **Finnish bookshops are always busy. Finns are avid readers and buy books in Swedish, German, and English, as well as in Finnish.**

Testament from the Bible into Finnish. He also wrote about traditional Finnish culture and religion.

The most famous Finnish writer of the nineteenth century was Elias Lönnrot, who compiled the *Kalevala*, a collection of poems, folk legends, and stories. The *Kalevala* is an epic, often compared to Homer's *Iliad*, in which history is combined with fiction, and a mythical, pastoral Finland comes to life. In this work, the Finns participate in the creation of the world.

Another famous writer of that century was Aleksis Kivi. His novel *Seven Brothers* was published in 1870 and has been translated into twenty languages. The story tells of seven brothers who reject civilization and live in the forests.

In the twentieth century, Mika Waltari became famous for *The Egyptian*, a historical novel about life in ancient Egypt. Frans Eemil Sillanpää, who wrote poetic novels about ordinary people, received the Nobel Prize for Literature in 1939. *The Unknown Soldier* by Väinö Linna was a best-seller after World War II. Veikko Huovinen's witty short stories are also popular in Finland.

Above: **Mikael Agricola is considered the father of Finnish literature.**

Arts

Theater and the arts flourish in Finland and are very much a part of its national pride and identity. Artists have searched for qualities and techniques that truly represent the Finnish spirit. They have found inspiration in the Finnish landscape, forests, and lakes and have portrayed the independent nature of the people. By far, the greatest inspiration in all art forms has come from the epic tales of the *Kalevala*.

While this national consciousness is evident in all aspects of the arts, artists have also been influenced by both the East and West because of Finland's geographical location and history of interaction with other nations. The result is a blend of cultural, national, and international influences.

In the 1890s, Finland began to chafe under Russian rule, and independence movements led to increased awareness of its identity as a nation. Interest in the *Kalevala* and Finnish folk

Below: **Street markets abound in Helsinki. The statue of the Three Smyths was created by Felix Nylund.**

poetry grew, and artists began to express their pride in and love of their country as a part of this nationalism. This golden age of Finnish art included Akseli Gallen-Kallela (1865–1931), whose paintings were inspired by the *Kalevala*. His pupil Hugo Simberg was known for his watercolor creations of Finnish folk tales, complete with devils and angels. The best paintings from this era can be found in museums all over Finland.

Finnish artists tend to prefer three-dimensional creations to paintings. Eila Hiltunen's monument to composer Jean Sibelius in Helsinki is made of chrome and metal tubes. The furniture designs of architect Alvar Aalto are both creative and functional, and Finnish glassware designers are internationally acclaimed. Sculptor Wäino Aaltonen (1894–1966) is probably most well-known for his 1952 statue of Paavo Nurmi, the Olympic runner. The statue shocked people when it was first unveiled because it depicts Nurmi running in the nude.

ARCHITECTURE

Finland is famous for its architects, who design modern, practical buildings that blend well with the environment. Alvar Aalto is probably the most well-known of all Finnish architects.

(A Closer Look, page 44)

Above: **Music appreciation begins at a young age in Finland.**

Music

Finland has produced many top conductors, singers, and musicians. A Finnish-born conductor and composer, Esa-Pekka Salonen has been world famous since the 1980s.

In summer, music events are held all over the country. Finns listen to all kinds of music, from classical to jazz to pop and rock. They learn to appreciate music at a young age, and music education is offered throughout Finland.

Finnish music began as traditional folk and church music. The first notable name in Finnish music was Fredrik Pacius (1809–1891), who composed the national anthem and the first Finnish opera, *The Hunt of King Charles.*

The greatest musician in Finland was composer Jean Sibelius (1865–1957). His music glorifies the Finns and expresses defiance against Russia. In Finland, Sibelius' most famous composition is the patriotic *Finlandia*, but he received international fame for the symphonies he composed and the contributions he made to the development of the symphony as an art form.

ROCK 'N' ROLL

Finnish rock 'n' roll is a unique blend of Western and Finnish cultures. Most rock bands sing in English, but the music is original and imaginative. In summer, festivals are held throughout the country, attracting up to 25,000 people. Leading bands from around the world perform at these rock festivals.

Theater and Dance

Finnish theater has its roots in ancient pagan folk rituals linked to hunting and fishing. The earliest known drama performance was staged in Turku in the 1650s. In the nineteenth century, a passion for theater spread throughout Finland. The first official theaters were built, and almost every local club and association had a theater for shows and poetry recitals.

Today, Finns are still avid theater fans, buying almost three million theater tickets a year. The scripts of about half the performances are written by Finns. Popular plays include those by Aleksis Kivi, Minna Canth, and Maria Jotuni. Finland currently has more than forty professional theater groups, as well as many amateur and youth theater groups.

Finns are also great fans of a variety of dance forms, from ballet to the tango to rock 'n' roll. Traditional folk dances are performed for special events and at outdoor festivals in summer. The Kuopio Dance and Music Festival is held every year to promote Finnish dance theater. Jorma Uotinen, the director of the Finnish National Ballet, is considered the most important figure in Finnish contemporary dance.

Below: Street musicians perform in the pedestrian zone in downtown Helsinki.

Leisure and Festivals

Enjoying the Great Outdoors

Finns love the great outdoors. They like to exercise, and they revel in the beauty of their country. The most popular summer sports include running, cycling, walking, swimming, golf, and tennis. Finnish families often spend entire weekends outdoors. Picnics are common, as are bird watching and picking mushrooms and wild berries in the forests.

The country's vast wilderness is wonderful for hiking and camping out, especially in summer. Many forests have well-marked trails and closely spaced footpaths, which make hiking easy even for the most inexperienced hiker. Twenty-nine nature reserves, covering almost one-third of the country, are fully equipped with camping facilities for overnight hikers.

Hunting is a favorite Finnish pastime in autumn. Hunters camp out in the forests and set traps for prey. Hare, deer, and birds are the most commonly hunted animals. Elks are hunted because they are plentiful and often cause road accidents.

PROTECTING THE FORESTS

Finland began to protect its forests in the nineteenth century. Nature reserves now cover nearly one-third of the country.
(*A Closer Look*, page 64)

Below: Hikers in Finland are rewarded with spectacular views.

Left: Children play outside on a glorious summer day.

Team Sports

Finland's national sport is *pesäpallo* (pay-SAH-PARL-loh), a variation of American baseball. It is widely played in rural areas and smaller towns in summer. The Finns also play soccer and ice hockey. The national soccer team's uniform is white with blue stripes, and Finland's best soccer player is Jari Litmanen.

The Olympics

Finland first entered the Olympic Games in 1906, and the country hosted the competitions in 1952. In 1906, Finland won the wrestling event. Since that time, the country has won a handful of medals at every Olympic competition.

Finland participates in many Olympic events, including water sports, but its most successful athletic events have been long-distance running and javelin throwing. The two most famous runners in Finland are Paavo Nurmi and Ville Ritola. Nurmi, the Flying Finn, won nine Olympic gold medals, while Ritola won five. In javelin throwing, Finland is a three-time Olympic medal winner.

FISHING AND WATER SPORTS

About 1.5 million Finns fish for fun, and nearly everyone enjoys some form of water sport. Finland offers sailing, white-water rafting, canoeing, and swimming.
(A Closer Look, page 52)

35

Winter Sports

Finnish winters are especially long, so winter sports, such as cross-country skiing, snowboarding, and ski jumping, are popular. Mass skiing events are held every weekend in winter, and thousands of Finns take part in the country's biggest cross-country skiing event, the 47-mile (75-km) Finlandia Race.

Another popular winter event is ice hockey. Finland has junior leagues for young players, and some outstanding players join professional teams in the United States. The best-known Finnish ice hockey players are Jari Kurri and Teemu Selänne. Finns play in the European National Hockey League, and Finland's Olympic team won a bronze medal in 1998.

Finns excel in other Olympic winter games as well. Harri and Marja-Liisa Kirvesniemi are famous cross-country skiers, who have been competing and winning medals for Finland for almost twenty years. In ski jumping, the most famous competitor is Olympic champion Matti Nykänen, who won gold medals in 1984 and 1988. Another medal winner in 1988 was long-distance skier Marjo Matikainen.

Winter sports in Finland also include ice sailing, ice skating, and ice fishing, or fishing through holes in the ice. Dogsled and reindeer races, snowmobile safaris, and competitions such as creating ice sculptures and roping reindeer are popular as well.

Above: **Cross-country skiing is only one of the many winter sports at which Finns excel.**

Car Racing

Some of Finland's biggest stars are in international auto racing. Two famous names are Mika Häkkinen and Tommi Mäkinen. Häkkinen won the prestigious Formula One race in 1998. Mäkinen was the world champion car rally driver from 1996 to 1998. Another famous racer is Ari Vatanen, who is also one of the newest Finnish members of the European Parliament.

Staying Indoors

When the cold season starts in Finland, many Finns turn to indoor activities. Reading is the most popular indoor activity, and bookstores and libraries are always busy in winter. Watching

television, surfing the Internet, and playing computer games are common activities among the younger generation. Finns are also avid collectors of dolls, stamps, coins, and matchbooks.

Above: **Reindeer races are popular in Lapland, where reindeer are raised as livestock.**

No matter how busy they are, Finns also find time for a cup of coffee at least three times a day. Cafés can be found all over Finland, even in libraries, theaters, and hairdressing salons. Afternoon coffee is usually enjoyed with buns, pastries, or cakes.

Cooking at home over the weekends is a family affair. Everyone helps prepare the meal, and baking cookies is very popular. Finns prefer a light, healthy diet and eat fish almost every day.

Left: **Finnish girls dress up as witches at Easter. They visit their neighbors to wish them well and receive candy in return.**

Easter

Easter celebrations in Finland are an interesting blend of Christian and pagan customs. Good Friday, the day of Christ's crucifixion, is more important to Finns than Easter, the day of Christ's resurrection. Easter is a time when Finns anticipate the coming of spring. Glorious music is played in churches, and people decorate their homes with pussy willow, dolls made of straw, and colored Easter eggs. Young girls also dress up as Easter witches.

May Day

Vappu (VAH-poo), or May Day, on May 1 is a national holiday that celebrates both Labor Day and the coming of spring in Finland. All businesses and factories are closed, and parades, concerts, street carnivals, and speeches mark the occasion.

MIDSUMMER BONFIRES

In the height of summer, Finns celebrate Midsummer Day. They light huge bonfires and stay up all night feasting, talking, singing, and dancing.
(A Closer Look, page 58)

Independence Day

Each year on December 6, Finns remember their fight for independence from Russian rule. Different parts of the country have their own celebrations to mark this day. In Helsinki, university students march with torches from the Hietaniemi Graveyard to Senate Square to honor those who sacrificed their lives for independence. Households display lit candles in windows to remember the heroes of Finnish independence. Shop windows are decorated in the national colors of blue and white, and cakes with blue and white icing are sold in bakeries.

Christmas Eve

On Christmas Eve, families rise early to prepare for the Christmas holiday. They decorate Christmas trees and bake special treats, such as *pipparkakku* (pee-PAHR-kah-koo), or ginger cookies. Toward noon, they gather in front of television sets for the government's traditional Christmas ceremony, and church bells ring throughout the country. Later, many families take a Christmas sauna together. Christmas Eve dinner includes ham, fish, and potato casserole, as well as *glogi* (GLUR-gee), a hot, spicy drink. On Christmas morning, families open gifts around the Christmas tree, attend church services, and celebrate the day together.

SANTA CLAUS

Santa Claus is said to live near the village of Rovaniemi in Lapland. He receives visitors from all over the world.
(A Closer Look, page 68)

Below: **Independence Day colors light up a park in Helsinki.**

Food

Finnish cuisine is a melting pot of influences from Russia and some parts of Scandinavia, particularly Sweden. Finns tend to eat simple, healthy food that is in season. For example, summer is the time for salmon, vegetables, and berries, while in autumn Finns eat wild mushrooms and meat, such as reindeer. One Finnish staple is fish, especially salmon, rainbow trout, and Finnish whitefish. Crayfish, a crustacean, is also a popular dish with Finns.

The traditional Finnish breakfast is porridge, which is eaten with milk and a pat of butter, but modern Finns prefer corn flakes, yogurt, toast, or rye bread with cheese and sausage. An all-time favorite is the Finnish *pulla* (POO-lah), bread made with cardamom and raisins and sprinkled with sugar.

Lunch, the main meal in Finland, is usually eaten in school or at work. It consists of salad, bread, and a main course of fish, chicken, or meat with sauce served with boiled potatoes, rice, or pasta. Finns have small dinners, which usually consist of some

Below: **Tempting displays of food attract shoppers to markets in Finland.**

easily prepared food that can be warmed in a microwave or by light frying. Popular choices include pizzas, hamburgers, casseroles, and fish sticks.

In Lapland, roasted or stewed reindeer is a typical dish. Two other Finnish favorites are *karjalanpaisti* (KAR-ee-LARN-pah-ih-ees-tee), a meat casserole, and *kalakukko* (KAH-lah-koo-koh), rye bread wrapped around fish and bacon.

Finns and Coffee

Finns are avid coffee drinkers. In fact, Finland is one of the top consumers of coffee per capita. The tradition of drinking coffee came to Finland in the middle of the eighteenth century. In 1767, the government tried unsuccessfully to ban coffee because it was thought to be an "unhealthy luxury drink." A century later, coffee drinking had spread throughout the country, from the city to the countryside. People drank it on Sundays after church and on festive celebrations, if not every day at home. Those who could not afford it mixed real coffee beans with rye, barley, or pea substitutes. By the beginning of the twentieth century, almost everyone in Finland was drinking coffee in the morning, afternoon, and evening.

SEAFOOD GALORE

Finns love to eat seafood, especially crayfish, a type of crustacean. They eat it smoked, raw, steamed, or fried. During crayfish season, Finns hold parties where only crayfish is served.

(A Closer Look, page 70)

A CLOSER LOOK AT FINLAND

Finns love their country's incredible forests and glorious lakes. In summer, they revel in its natural beauty — hiking, fishing, and celebrating events outdoors. In winter, deep snow and frozen lakes create a vast, silent landscape, and long polar nights are often brilliant with light from the aurora borealis.

Finland is a modern, technologically advanced country. Women's rights and protecting the environment are important issues. The well-educated and hardworking Finns also have given the world the most advanced communications systems.

Opposite: **Lasso-the-reindeer contests are held in Lapland every winter.**

Pioneers in design, Finns treasure their architectural heritage as well. Both their solid medieval castles and soaring, modernist buildings reflect the nationalistic, yet down-to-earth nature of the Finnish people. Their creativity and imagination are also evident in fashionable ceramics and glassware.

These sophisticated, reserved Europeans jump in the snow after a sauna, swim in lakes filled with ice, and claim to have the real Santa Claus living in their country. Although they are generally light, healthy eaters, when crayfish season comes, they have parties at which all they do is eat and drink!

Above: **Hikers take in a view of Finland's wilderness forests, from mountains in the far northeast.**

Architecture

Finnish architecture has undergone a transition from Swedish- and Russian-influenced styles to universal modernism. Finland's architecture today reflects the modernist and functionalist movements of the twentieth century. The style is imaginative and distinctly Finnish. Finnish architects design buildings that are functional and blend well with the environment.

Finns treasure their architectural monuments, both old and new. Medieval castles have been refurbished and are used as concert halls or museums. Churches and cathedrals, monuments to the development of architecture in the nineteenth and twentieth centuries, are still used for worship services. The newer creations are modern and daring, as stunning in their way as the older buildings. Temppeliaukio Church, built in 1969 in Helsinki, was carved into a solid-rock hill, and only its copper dome is visible from the street.

Below: **The Helsinki railway station was designed by Eliel Saarinen in 1916. Many designers have copied its Gothic style, including those who created a similar building for the movie *Batman*.**

Finnish Designers

Eliel Saarinen (1873–1950), a pioneer in Finnish architecture, designed buildings both in Finland and the United States. The National Museum and railway station in Helsinki are imaginative but functional buildings that reflect Finnish nationalism and love of nature.

Alvar Aalto (1898–1976) and Erik Bryggman (1891–1955) blended architecture and landscape in their designs for public buildings. Combining modern styles with Finland's historical traditions, they revolutionized the country's architecture in the twentieth century. The beauty of Aalto's work lay in how he expressed the relationship between humans, nature, and buildings. He practiced "organic architecture," designing buildings that suit both their environments and their purposes. He designed Turku's Paimio Sanatorium and Villa Mairea, a fine example of modern architecture in a private residence. Finlandia Hall in Helsinki is a creative yet functional concert hall that features white marble and black granite. A versatile artist, he also designed furniture, glassware, and even jewelry.

Above: **Temppeliaukio Church in Helsinki is carved into the side of a hill. Only the copper dome is visible from the outside. Tuomo and Timo Suomalainen designed the church in 1969.**

Communications Superpower

Finland has a long tradition in developing technological skills and training, and the country has achieved much success in the area of high technology. Finland was one of the first countries in the world to set up a telephone service and is known for its spectacular growth in the field of mobile communications. A number of Finnish companies are prominent in the worldwide telecommunications equipment market.

Finland has the highest percentage of mobile telephone users in the world. More than 60 percent of Finns owned mobile telephones in 1999, a record-breaking number. In a country with just over five million people, there are 3.1 million mobile telephone users; that is more than the number of fixed-line telephone connections.

Below: **Young children in Finland do not really have mobile phones, but just about everyone else does.**

Left: Finns use the Internet for home banking and for information services related to education, public transportation, weather, and entertainment.

Nokia

The flagship of Finnish communications is Oy Nokia Ab, the largest manufacturer of mobile telephones in the world. Although its name may sound Japanese, Nokia is purely Finnish. The company started as a small pulp mill and grew into a large conglomerate, producing rubber products, plastics, consumer electronics, and computers. In 1972, Nokia and Telecom Finland jointly launched the world's first regular mobile telephone service. By 1991, Nokia was producing both telephones and network support equipment for digital cellular mobile communications throughout the world.

Computers and the Internet

The Internet market in Finland is also a fast-growing communications sector. Finland is one of the most enthusiastic users of the Internet. For the past few years, it continuously has been ranked first in the world in the use of computer networks and the Internet. The number of computers linked to the Internet doubles annually in Finland, and, in 1999, the country had half a million Internet connections.

Below: Nokia telecommunications research center designs digital cellular telephones.

47

Etiquette

Talking

In Finland, the spoken word is as important as the written. An old Finnish proverb says, "Take a man by his word and a bull by its horn." Finns think carefully about what they want to say and expect others to do the same. They take verbal agreements and contracts very seriously. Finns are good listeners, and they consider it impolite to interrupt someone who is talking. They usually speak at a slow pace and do not chat easily with strangers or new acquaintances.

Greetings

When introducing themselves, Finns usually state their first names first, followed by their surnames. They are particular about their professional titles and expect to be addressed by them — for example, Doctor Mikkonen, Architect Leino, Director Virtanen. When two Finns first meet, they shake hands, make eye contact, and nod the head, even with children. Often, a man will raise his hat in greeting. Embracing in public is rare, although a kiss on the cheek is common among female friends.

Below: Finns tend to be formal with strangers but relax over coffee with friends.

48

Visiting Finns

In Finland, the home is very much the focus of social life. Finns often invite friends and business associates home for dinner. They like to cook and prefer to eat and drink in the comfort of the home. The atmosphere is often relaxed and informal. Guests are expected to remove their shoes before entering a house and bring a bouquet of flowers or bottle of wine for the host or hostess.

Finns also invite guests to their summer cottages. Although these cottages often have no electricity, running water, or flushing toilets, guests are expected to appreciate "roughing it." Guests should dress casually and practically and offer to help with routine chores.

Telephone Manners

Mobile telephones are widely used in Finland, but they are not allowed on airplanes or in hospitals. Finns consider it barbaric to use a telephone at a concert, in a theater, or in church. It is also not appropriate to receive calls during meetings.

Above: **A gift of flowers or chocolate is greatly appreciated when visitors are invited to a Finn's home.**

Finnish Sauna: A National Tradition

Finns love their saunas. Friends or family members often relax in the sauna after a hard day's work, talking over the day in the steamy warmth.

Finns believe that a sauna cleanses the body and rejuvenates the soul. Finland has more than one and a half million saunas, which are used at least once a week by family and friends. Most apartment buildings have common saunas, and public saunas are widely available in Finland. Often, when Finns move to a new home or a different country, one of the first changes they make is to build a sauna.

Today, the sauna is used only for bathing, but in the past it was sometimes a place where women gave birth and doctors treated patients, because it was the cleanest place in the home. Sauna bathing is a tradition that has evolved through the years. The earliest saunas were holes dug in the ground with heated stones in the middle. People would cover themselves with animal hides and sit around the stones. No one really knows who started the sauna tradition, but many Finns believe it was their ancestors.

Above: **Sauna bathers often gently beat each other with birch branches as a massage and as a means of increasing blood circulation.**

Left: **Although public saunas are usually segregated, women and men bathe together when among close friends and families.**

Saunas Today

A typical sauna today consists of a small enclosed room with two wooden benches and an electric stove filled with fist-sized stones. It also has a bench and a dressing room. The more traditional saunas, usually found in lakeside summer cabins, may have a bench and a wood-fueled stove for heating. Bathers cool off in the lake and sometimes in the snow!

Finns sometimes bathe together in the nude, but this is not a rule. Some wear a towel or a bathing suit. Bathers basically sit back and relax. Sometimes they gently beat their bodies with fresh birch branches to increase blood circulation. To turn up the heat, water is thrown on the stones. The water vaporizes quickly, letting off hot, moist air. The temperature in a sauna ranges from 140° to 230° F (60° to 110° C).

Although many people around the world enjoy saunas today, Finns are undoubtedly the most enthusiastic sauna bathers. Many Finns believe that a house without a sauna is not a home.

Above: **While most Finns shower after a sauna in winter, the more daring jump into an icy lake to cool off.**

Fishing and Water Sports

With two seas, hundreds of rivers, and thousands of lakes, Finland is an ideal place for fishing and water sports. These leisure activities are very popular among Finns as well as tourists. The best times for fishing in Finland are spring and autumn, although some people fish throughout the year.

Finns practice many different styles of fishing — angling, fly fishing, and using nets. Favorite weekend activities are fishing in the lakes and then pan frying the catches for dinner. Sometimes Finns go out on the open sea and fish from boats. Many kinds of fish can be found in Finnish waters. The most common fish are perch, cod, whitefish, rainbow trout, sea trout, salmon, and Atlantic herring.

Although licenses are required for some sport fishing in summer, every Finn has the right to fish in winter. A few areas,

Below: **Friends shoot the rapids in a wilderness park in Lapland.**

Left: A fisherman hauls in his nets and catch of the day.

however, are off-limits, such as protected water zones and places near private homes.

Fishing through the ice over lakes is the most popular form of winter fishing. Finns first cut holes in the ice. Then they drop in a baited line and try to attract fish by gently jerking the line. If the water is clear, the fish can see the bait from dozens of yards away.

Water Sports

In summer, it is not uncommon to see the sails of yachts and dinghies flying just above the waters of Finland's lakes and open seas. The prime sailing region is around the islands near Turku. Canoeing, kayaking, and rowing are favorite water sports, and white-water rafting is common in Lapland and along the northeastern border.

Every July, the Sulkava Rowing Regatta, near Savonlinna, draws ten thousand participants. In winter, Finns sail on the frozen lakes, and the All Saints Ice Regatta is held in Rovaniemi.

TREKKING AND FISHING IN LAPLAND

Lapland is a popular place for trekking and fishing. Every year, thousands of people fill their backpacks and disappear into the woods. In recent years, Lapland has opened up more areas for fishing. Arctic char and salmon are the best catches.

Land of the Midnight Sun

The sun never sets in summer in northern Finland. Lapland, the area covering the extreme north of Finland, is known as the Land of the Midnight Sun. From mid-May until the end of July, the sun stays above the horizon twenty-four hours a day.

The southern regions of Finland do not experience a midnight sun, but it is never completely dark at night there, either. Instead, the evening light remains in the sky long enough to merge with the first light of morning. During summer, Finland gets many visitors who want to experience Lapland's midnight sun, as well as its boundless forests and vast landscape.

After many days with no darkness, the area experiences a fifty-day "sunset," when days are short and the sky gets dark quickly. Following this is Kaamos, when the sun "disappears," and even noontime is filled with darkness. This is the time when spectacular lights dance across the midnight sky.

Below: **Nature is at its most awesome when the sun hides for the long Finnish winters.**

Northern Lights

Called northern lights, or aurora borealis, these flashes of light are the result of electrically charged particles traveling at great speeds and colliding with one another in the sky. This phenomenon occurs about two hundred nights a year in Lapland, at a height of 62 miles (100 km) above the ground.

Northern lights are yellowish green, with a tinge of red above the green. Each flash has a unique shape and is different from the previous one.

The aurora, which means "dawn of the day," occurs in both the Arctic and Antarctic regions. In the Antarctic, the lights are called the polar aurora. Finland's lights are known as aurora borealis, after the Greek god of the north wind, Boreas.

Northern lights actually occur in summer as well, but they are seldom seen during that season because the sky is never dark enough. The best time to view these lights is on a late winter evening in northern Lapland. One of the best places to see them is from the Arctic Academy, just outside Sodankylä.

Above: Even Turku, in the far south, has days of almost complete darkness in the winter months. Here, the lights surrounding Turku Cathedral stay on all day.

Medieval Castles

Medieval castles are some of the oldest architectural monuments in Finland. They were built of solid stone by the Swedish and were used as fortresses to defend Finland from invaders. Castles also served as centers of administration and taxation. By the beginning of the sixteenth century, however, they had become outdated for defense purposes because firearms had become too powerful. A century later, the castles were turned into barracks, prisons, warehouses, and grain stores.

Finland's medieval castles were never pulled down or rebuilt. Their foundations were made of solid natural stone, mostly granite, so it was not worth the effort. Instead, they remain "phantoms of the past." After World War II, some castles were restored and renovated. They are used as museums and for cultural activities.

Below: The oldest sections of Häme Castle date back to the 1260s, when it was a fortified camp. Later, it became the residence of great nobles and then an outpost of Swedish royalty.

Left: **Olavinlinna Castle was built in 1475 by the Russians, who occupied the eastern part of Finland from 1323 until 1808, when they took possession of the entire country. The castle is on a small island and is reached by a rotating bridge.**

Three Phantoms of the Past

Turku was the original capital of Finland, and Turku Castle is its largest medieval structure. The castle was built in 1280, in the form of a rectangular camp with four gates. Before the end of the sixteenth century, the castle had survived nine sieges. Swedish monarchs used this castle as a residence when they visited Finland. Today, Turku Castle is a popular attraction in Finland. Every room, object, and painting represents some aspect of Finland's history.

Häme Castle was built in Hämeenlinna, just north of Helsinki, in the 1290s. This brick and stone castle formed part of a defense line against attacks from the Russians in the east. Later, it was used as an administrative center and then as a granary and prison. Today, Häme Castle houses several exhibition halls of the Finnish National Museum.

Olavinlinna Castle, a three-towered medieval fortress in Savonlinna, was built in 1475 to mark the Finnish-Russian border. Today, Olavinlinna Castle is home to the annual Savonlinna Opera Festival.

Midsummer Bonfires

At the height of summer, when the sun never sets, Finns celebrate Midsummer Day, a festival of light. They feast, sing, and dance around bonfires, delighting in the longest day of the year.

Many traditional beliefs are associated with Midsummer, or *Juhannus* (yu-HAH-nohs). Pagan worshipers believed that this particular day marked the end of summer and the approach of winter. As the god of summer was challenged by the god of winter, pagans lit bonfires to worship the healing and purifying powers of light. The light was intended to help the god of summer drive off the god of winter.

Christians once believed that this was the day when the doors of hell opened, letting out spirits and ghosts to roam Earth. Bonfires were lit to purify the air and keep the spirits from doing any harm. Others believed that Midsummer was linked to the magic of the nightless day. For farmers, Midsummer was a break between the planting and harvesting seasons.

Below: **Huge bonfires are lit to celebrate Midsummer Day.**

Whatever the origins of Midsummer Day, it remains a celebration of summer. Because of their long and cold winters, Finns are especially appreciative of the flowers, fresh fruit, and long, balmy days of this season. Midsummer is a day to acknowledge the glory of nature, and Finns do this by flying their national flag everywhere, decorating Midsummer poles and boats with flowers, and performing folk dances.

The bonfire is the high point of the celebration. The fire lends an air of festivity to the occasion. Finns stack up twigs and wood in the shape of a hill, then set fire to it. In the old days, every village would build its own bonfire.

Finns like to celebrate Midsummer near the sea or by their lakes, rather than in big cities. More than two-thirds of Finns live in the city, but they go to the countryside during this season. Although there are huge public bonfires, many Finns go to their isolated summer cottages in the forests or by the lakes and build their own bonfires. They take saunas, eat and drink, and stay up all night talking, dancing, and singing traditional folk songs around the bonfire.

Above: **Folk dances and other performances take place throughout the day. At night, informal dancing and songs around the bonfires are fun for all.**

Modern Design

Finland's furniture, jewelry, and textile designs are unique. Their clean, modern lines have a timeless, classic quality, and their creations are not only beautiful, but practical as well. Chrome and plastic are often used with natural materials, such as wood, glass, ceramics, fabric, and metal. Geometric shapes and strong splashes of color are also seen in Finnish design.

Finnish design was first introduced at the Paris World Exhibition in 1900, but it did not become a household word until the 1950s and 1960s. The designs are popular because they are artistic, yet useful. The furniture is sleek and functional. The intricately woven rugs are practical and durable. Simple household items, such as pots and pans, tools, and textiles, come in creative shapes and imaginative colors. Finnish designers and inventors also have developed biodegradable shopping bags and created tools for doctors, such as surgical "gloves" that have a light at the tip of each finger.

Above: **Alvar Aalto's classic Savoy vase is said to be a reflection of the lakes of Finland.**

Left: **A Finnish worker manufactures decorative glass at the Nuutajarvi Glassworks, which specializes in functional, artistic glassware.**

Inspired by Nature

Finns draw their inspiration and materials from nature, mostly from forests, lakes, and the changing seasons. Wood is the most popular material for furniture, while textiles vary in style and color, from the subtle pastels of the south to the dynamic reds and blues of Lapland. The rugs have scenes of the seasons, and glass designs are often based on Finnish flora and fauna.

Glassworks factories have been in Finland for over two centuries. Today, they produce some of the world's most prestigious household porcelain and ceramics. Alvar Aalto's Savoy vase, created in 1936, is a classic item that is reproduced in many sizes and colors. The factories, however, keep abreast of changing styles and fashion and introduce new designs to please their cosmopolitan market.

Some designers look to the *Kalevala* for inspiration. The jewelry firm Kalevala-Koru is famous for its animal motifs, such as reindeer, bear, and fish designs. Finns also make elegant jewelry and ornaments from recycled paper.

Above: **Carpets and other textiles often depict scenes of Finland.**

Money Grows on Trees

If money could grow on trees, the first dollars would sprout in Finland. Forests cover about three-fourths of the country, and they are Finland's most important natural resource. Besides being a major source of export revenue, the country's forests are closely linked with its history and culture. The Finnish bond with forests is expressed in Finnish literature, paintings, music, photography, and architecture.

More than 400,000 people own a plot of forestland, and everyone has the right of access. About a third of the forestland belongs to the government, and another 10 percent is owned by

Below: Logs are transported by water and truck to factories that process them into pulp and paper for export.

wood-processing companies. The forests provide a place for leisure activities. Hunters roam the forests looking for elk and grouse. On weekends, families gather berries and pick mushrooms. Hiking, camping, and survival-type activities are popular as well.

When Finland first became independent, the new nation's economy was built on the forest industry, which accounted for 80 to 90 percent of its export revenues. Today, the volume of trees growing every year exceeds the amount felled because a strict conservation policy is enforced. However, pulp, paper, and timber still make up 40 percent of Finland's total exports.

Agriculture

Finland is the world's northernmost country in which arable farming is practiced, although the climate is not always favorable. Traditionally, agriculture and forestry were Finland's main sources of income. The farmers would work in the fields in summer, then do forestry work and sell timber in winter.

The introduction of mechanization and land reform in the 1950s improved existing farms and eliminated nonproductive ones. As a result, Finland has fewer and smaller farms today. The average farm has about 33 acres (13.4 hectares) of arable land. Only about 7 percent of the Finnish workforce makes a living from agriculture, and only about 8 percent of the land is under cultivation.

Most Finnish farms are in southwestern Finland. This region has the mildest climate, the best soil, and the fewest trees in the country. Finland's most important crops are wheat, barley, oats, potatoes, and sugar beets. The country grows these crops only for its own use and not for export.

Some farms raise livestock, which includes cattle, hogs, sheep, and horses, while other farms specialize in poultry. The Sami in the north raise reindeer as draft animals and for their meat and hides. Raising livestock accounts for two-thirds of the national income from farming.

Above: **A typical Finnish agricultural farm has small haystacks and wooden farm buildings.**

Protecting the Forests

Finns view their forested land as both a symbol of national pride and a source of income. As early as 1886, a Forestry Act protected the forests and endangered wildlife in Finland. In 1938, the Finnish Environment Protection Association was founded to establish nature reserves and preserve rare plants. Today, the association has 170 branches around the country. In 1991, the Finnish government introduced the Wilderness Act to protect the greenery in Lapland. Today, twelve different areas are protected, making up nearly one-third of Lapland. Forest activities are restricted in these areas, and no felling of trees is allowed.

Environmental Damage

Forest products, such as timber and paper, are important exports, but the manufacturing of these products can cause great environmental damage. Deforestation, or the clearing of trees, spoils the natural environment and affects animals living in the

Below: **Heavily forested parks, such as this one near Tampere, are abundant in Western Finland.**

Left: **Eurasian brown bears, which are similar to North American grizzly bears, are protected animals in Finland because only a few hundred of the species remain.**

forests. The government's solution is a responsible forest management plan, with incentives to encourage private forest owners to follow it.

Forests are also facing destruction from acid rain, which is caused by a combination of rain and toxic wastes in the air. Finland has already set legal limits to control industrial waste emission, but environmentalists want even tighter controls.

The government is also trying to control litter in the forests. Finnish forests are popular hiking destinations, and careless people destroy natural beauty by breaking branches, building fires, and littering.

Green policies, especially recycling schemes, have long been part of everyday Finnish life. The Finns also try to find new ways to introduce environment-friendly designs. They pioneered the idea of using chopped-up car tires to make roads. They also conduct research on biodegradable plastic, especially for shopping bags. Finnish designers advocate the use of recycled and recyclable materials instead of raw materials. They also encourage minimal use of energy in the manufacturing process and longer product lives.

Sami, the Native People of Finland

The Sami are some of Finland's earliest settlers. Their origins are obscure, but their Finno-Ugric language indicates that they were part of a general migration west from Russia about 6,000 years ago. The early Sami community consisted of small groups scattered throughout Finland, but as other settlers moved in, the Sami shifted to the north. Today, there are about 70,000 Sami in the world, and some 6,000 live in Finland, mostly in Lapland, the northernmost part of Finland.

Sometimes called the reindeer people, the Sami are nomads at heart. They once lived off the land and wandered from place to place, hunting, fishing, and herding reindeer. The reindeer remains an important source of income. It provides milk and meat and pulls sleighs to transport goods. Its skin is used to make tents

WHY ARE LAPPS NOW CALLED SAMI?

The Sami of Finland used to be called Lapps. In Swedish, a *lapp* is a patch of cloth used for mending, which implies that the Sami wear patched clothes. So, today, Sami is the correct term to use.

Left: Traditional Sami clothes are combinations of bright-colored fabrics and reindeer hides.

Above: **Sami gather outside a kota. Traditional kota were made from reindeer hides.**

and clothes, while its fur is turned into shoes, gloves, leggings, and coats. Its antlers are often carved into sculptures to be sold.

The Sami have managed to preserve their culture and traditions. Their language, traditional clothing, handicrafts, and music are all distinctively different from other ethnic groups in Scandinavia. They traditionally lived in a *kota* (KOH-tah), a tent shaped like the North American teepee. Reindeer skin covered the tent and kept the tent floor warm.

Today, many Sami pursue careers that do not relate to their cultural heritage, but almost every family has at least one member who is still involved with raising reindeer. Many Sami like to wear their traditional, bright-colored clothing because it is an expression of ethnicity and togetherness.

The Finnish government recognizes the Sami as a separate ethnic group. In 1973, the Sami in Finland were allowed to form their own parliament, which provides a forum for promoting Sami concerns. Finland's Sami also have their own publications, theater, and arts.

Santa Claus

The Santa Claus Legend

Many children are familiar with Santa Claus and know him as a big, jolly man with a long, flowing beard, wearing a red suit, and laughing as he shouts, "Ho ho ho!" This image of Santa Claus became popular in North America in the nineteenth century. The Santa Claus legend, however, actually began in Europe.

The original Santa is believed to be Bishop Nicholas of Myra, in western Turkey, who lived in the fourth century A.D. Bishop Nicholas was known for his keen interest in helping poor and unhappy children. After his death, he was buried in his church at Myra, but his remains were stolen in the eleventh century A.D. by Italian sailors who took them to Bari, in Italy. The popularity of Saint Nicholas grew among Christians in Europe. He was the patron saint of Greece in the Middles Ages, and in England, he was called Father Christmas. The Dutch call him *Sinterklaas*, from which we get his English name, *Santa Claus*.

Below: **The Santa Claus Village, near Rovaniemi, receives about a half million visitors each year.**

Over the years, Finland has come to be known as the "Home of Santa Claus," and there are many legends about him. Finns believe that he fell in love with Lapland and decided to make it his permanent home. It is said that every Christmas, Santa delivers gifts to children on a sleigh pulled by reindeer. Many children believe that Santa Claus and his wife live with dozens of hardworking elves, who help them make all the gifts. They are the only ones who can enter his magical home. The Sami who live near Santa's home know him as someone who is always ready to help any person or animal in need.

Above: **Children from all over the world come to visit Santa Claus in his village near Rovaniemi, Finland.**

Santa Claus Village

In Finland today, the Santa Claus Village lies near the town of Rovaniemi on the Arctic Circle. Children from around the world come here to visit with Santa and his reindeer.

In the village, visitors can have their Christmas cards postmarked with "Santa Claus Village." Some 500,000 tourists visit this village each year, and over 700,000 letters addressed to "Santa Claus, North Pole" are delivered here annually.

Seafood Galore

Thanks to Finland's thousands of lakes and two seas, a wide variety of fresh seafood is always available in the country. The Finns eat seafood at home, in restaurants, on festive occasions, and at cookouts around campfires. Fish is a standard item on the Finnish dining table. It is served smoked, grilled, roasted, or in a pie. Finns also like marinated or salted raw fish and fish soup, especially *lohikeitto* (LOH-ih-KAY-ee-toh), or salmon soup. Different kinds of roe, or fish eggs, are typically served with toast, sour cream, and minced onions.

Seasonal Fish

Some fish are only available at certain times of the year. In the beginning of the year, the best catch is burbot, which has delicious roe. Summer is the season for perch, pike, bream, salmon, and whitefish, while Baltic herring is the best catch in October.

Below: **Fish roasted over an open fire are tasty treats for campers.**

Left: **Cooking crayfish for annual parties is quite a feat since one person can easily eat up to twelve crayfish at one sitting.**

Herring and icy drinks are a must for May Day morning. On Christmas Day, lunch begins with cold cuts of fish served with salads and boiled potatoes. Herring is in the dressings and garnishes, and slightly salted salmon and roe are served as well.

Finns crave crayfish, or *rapu* (RAH-poo), which look and taste like small lobsters. Since the crayfish season is only from the end of July to the beginning of September, Finns always find out in advance exactly when and where the best crayfish will be available. On the first day of the season, gourmets will pay almost any price to devour the delicacy, but the price tends to fall later in the season if the catch is good.

Crayfish parties are held throughout the country, both at home and in restaurants. At home, the feast begins in late afternoon with huge servings of steaming crayfish. Finns eat, drink, and sing late into the night.

Women in Finland

Unemployed women are rare in Finland. Most women have careers that continue after they are married and have children. In fact, women make up almost half the Finnish workforce. Women have equal opportunities for education and employment. In accordance with the Equality Act of 1987, gender discrimination in the workplace is against the law, but women's salaries are still 25 percent lower than those of men.

Women's Achievements

In 1870, Maria Tschetsulin was the first woman to pass the entrance examination for a university. Eight years later, Rosina Heikel was the first woman in Scandinavia to graduate with a degree in medicine. Today, some 60 percent of all doctors in Finland are women.

In 1906, Finnish women were the first in Europe to be granted the right to vote and be members of parliament. In 1907, nineteen women were elected into parliament, and over 30 percent of the current members are women. Women also serve in United Nations (U.N.) peacekeeping operations, and they have been allowed to volunteer for military service since 1995.

Below: **Finnish women serve in North Atlantic Treaty Organization (NATO) and U.N. peacekeeping missions to Bosnia and African nations.**

In 2000, Foreign Minister Tarja Halonen made history by becoming the first elected woman president of Finland. The candidate of the Social Democratic Party, she won 51.6 percent of the votes cast in the February election. Her election was a victory for the women of Finland.

In the arts, soloist Karita Mattila was chosen to represent Finland at the worldwide millennium New Year concert. Modernist composer Kaija Saariaho is known throughout the world. Playwright Minna Canth was a pioneer of the feminist movement in the 1880s. In 1991, the National Theater appointed a woman director for the first time in its 100-year history.

FINNISH WELFARE

The welfare system in Finland provides good-quality, heavily subsidized child care programs. Women who wish to return to the workforce when their children are infants can easily find good child care centers and nursery schools.

RELATIONS WITH NORTH AMERICA

Relations between Finland and North America began before Finland was an independent nation. Many Finns emigrated to North America in the nineteenth century when their country was part of Russia. These Finns settled mainly in Michigan, Minnesota, and Massachusetts. Emigration continued into the twentieth century but fell off after Finland became an independent nation in 1917.

Although the United States traded with Finland, most North Americans did not know much about Finland until 1939. At this time, the Soviet Union invaded Finland because it wanted more

Opposite: **Snoopy, a popular American comic-strip character, is a familiar figure in Finland. Here, he is featured at a children's playground in Savonlinna.**

land as a buffer against German aggression. The Finns fought back with great courage, bringing the Soviet army almost to a standstill. They lost the war but won the admiration of the American people. Since then, North America and Finland have been trading partners and have worked together for world peace.

Finland today has been called the most Americanized country in Europe. American movies, music, books, food, and clothing are all popular. In the United States and Canada, the opposite has taken place — there has been a revival of Finnish culture and customs.

Above: **U.S. president Bill Clinton (*left*), Finnish president Martti Ahtisaari (*center*), and Russian president Boris Yeltsin discuss peacekeeping measures in Bosnia at the Helsinki Summit in March 1997.**

International Cooperation

Finland's status as a neutral country has meant that opposing countries can meet in Helsinki to work out differences. During the Cold War (1945–1990), when the United States and the Soviet Union were politically and economically opposed, Finland remained neutral. Its 1948 Treaty of Friendship, Cooperation, and Mutual Assistance ensured good relations with the Soviet Union, and trade with the United States continued as well.

From 1969 to 1972, Finland hosted the Strategic Arms Limitation Talks between the Soviet Union and the United States. In 1972, the international Conference on Security and Cooperation in Europe (CSCE) met in Finland, and the final agreement was signed by the United States, Canada, and thirty-three European countries in Helsinki in 1975.

Finland has cooperated with the United States and Canada through various international organizations, such as the United Nations (UN), the CSCE, and the Organization for Economic Cooperation and Development (OECD). Finland has been involved in both UN and North Atlantic Treaty Organization

Below: **Finnish soldiers participate in peacekeeping missions around the world. These troops are on their way to Kosovo.**

(NATO) peacekeeping operations in the Middle East and Bosnia. It also participates in U.N. programs for developing nations, especially in Africa.

Above: **World leaders meet in Helsinki in August 1975. They are (*left to right*) British prime minister Harold Wilson, U.S. president Gerald Ford, French president Valéry Giscard D'Estaing, and German chancellor Helmut Schmidt.**

Current Relations

A friendly relationship between the United States and Finland has developed in the years since World War II. After the war, the United States provided loans through the Marshall Plan, a U.S. aid program for war-torn nations. These loans helped rebuild Finland's economy and spirit. Since that time, Finland has grown to become a key player in negotiations between countries, as well as providing a neutral location where countries can meet.

Finnish presidents Urho Kekkonen and Mauno Koivisto have both paid state visits to the United States. Several U.S. presidents, including Gerald Ford and Bill Clinton, have visited Finland during their terms of office. The Finnish American Chamber of Commerce promotes trade and investment between Finland and the United States. It has members in banking, finance, law, accounting, manufacturing, transportation, and consultancy.

Shared Concerns and Trade

The United States and Finland share deep interests in the political and economic development of Russia and the Baltic states. Both countries are also involved in helping developing nations, especially in Africa and Southeast Asia.

In 1999, Finland was the president of the European Union for the first time. During its term, Finland promoted transatlantic ties with the United States and worked on resolving trade disputes between the United States and Europe.

Trade between the countries has always been important, and the United States is Finland's fourth largest trading partner, both in imports and exports, after Germany, Sweden, and the United Kingdom. In 1998, Finland imported U.S. $2.7 billion worth of goods from the United States and exported U.S. $3.2 billion.

Some famous Finnish company names in North America are Nokia, the electronics and telecommunications giant, and Kone, the elevator manufacturer. Finnish products in America include paper machines and forest tractors.

Opposite: **Finnish inventions contribute to good relations between Finland and other developed countries. These surgical gloves, a Finnish invention, have tiny lights at the tip of each finger.**

Below: **Prime Minister Paavo Lipponen was spokesperson for Finland during the country's 1999 half-year term as president of the European Union.**

Early Settlers in America

Long before Finland was an independent country, Finns emigrated to North America. The first known group came to the American colonies in 1638 and founded New Sweden on the Delaware River. Later, Finns came as part of a Scandinavian movement from the Old World (Europe) to the New World (America), which lasted from about 1860 to 1920.

Finns came in search of land, political stability, and a higher standard of living. In all, about 300,000 Finns came to the United States between 1864 and 1914, and another 20,000 settled in Canada during this time.

The first big group of Finnish immigrants settled in Minnesota. Soon after, more immigrants arrived in the mining areas of Michigan, which became another popular destination for Finnish immigrants.

Finns also settled in New York and Massachusetts. Later, they spread westward to Montana, California, Oregon, and Washington. Those who went to Canada mostly settled in Ontario and on the West Coast.

MILITARY RELATIONS

Finns have fought alongside Americans since the mid-nineteenth century, when Finnish immigrants in the United States were soldiers in the American Civil War (1861–1865). In the twentieth century, Finnish military personnel joined the U.S. Special Forces and airborne troops to fight in World War II. Finns also wrote a winter warfare manual for the U.S. Army, based on their experiences fighting the Russians in dense forests and deep snow.

Impact on North American Life

Initially, Finns lived in places where they could find jobs similar to those they had back home. Tailors and craftsmen went to New York, Boston, and Chicago. Sailors looked for work in harbor towns. Fishermen went to Washington and Oregon. Some found work in the copper mines of Michigan, gold and silver mines of South Dakota, and coal mines of Montana and Wyoming. Those who went to California worked in gold fields or on fruit farms. Finnish women became maids for wealthy families on the East Coast or worked in textile factories.

In 1862, the U.S. government offered free land in the Midwest to anyone who would farm and live on it for five years. Many Finns took advantage of this offer, and settlements grew in Minnesota, Michigan, and Wisconsin, states that were similar in terrain and climate to their home country. By 1920, about 25 percent of the Finns in North America made their living from farming. The communities grew, and Finns were known as people who were hardworking and reliable.

FINLAND, MINNESOTA

The American village of Finland is in Lake County, in the far northeastern corner of Minnesota. The county has dense forests, a northern climate, and is near a huge lake — Lake Superior. Many of its residents are descendants of Finnish immigrants. They celebrate Finnish festivals and enjoy many Finnish outdoor activities.

Below: Organic strawberries grown by Finns in the United States and Finland are a hit with everyone.

Although Finns made up only one percent of Europeans who emigrated during these years, they had a significant impact on North America. Most Finns were Lutheran, and the Finnish Evangelical Lutheran Church was established in 1890 in Calumet, Michigan. It maintained close ties with the state church of Finland, and services were in the Finnish language until the 1960s. By the early twentieth century, there were about one hundred Lutheran congregations in North America. In 1962, the Finnish Lutheran Church merged with other Lutheran churches to become the Lutheran Church in America. In 1988, this church united with two other churches to form the Evangelical Lutheran Church in America.

Finns were also known for their cooperative approach to farming and labor unions. They believed, and still believe, in organizations and government policies that support the social needs of people, such as health and education programs, good working conditions, and social security. They set up the Finnish Workers Society in Minnesota in 1903 and the nationwide Finnish Socialist Federation in 1906.

Above: **Mummers' Parades take place on New Year's Day in Philadelphia, Pennsylvania. The participants wear elaborate costumes and dance in the streets. This celebration dates back to the 1640s, when Swedish and Finnish immigrants in the United States celebrated the New Year in this way.**

Above: **Producer Renny Harlin (*right*) and actress Geena Davis discuss their film *Speechless*.**

Ethnic Pride

The early Finnish communities were active in sports, drama, and music. The first Finnish newspaper was published in 1876. Many other newspapers followed, and immigrants were able to keep in touch with all the news of their homeland. They kept most of their cultural traditions and celebrated Finnish festivals, such as Midsummer Day.

As the years passed, though, the early Finnish-American organizations lost their importance. Their culture became American culture and their language English. Finnish children went to American schools, and even the most traditional Finns began to feel more American than Finnish.

In the late 1960s, Finnish-Americans were caught up in a surge of ethnic pride that arose among Americans of European ancestry. Sauna and sisu were once more known as symbols of the unique Finnish culture. Today, the Finns in North America keep their culture alive in many ways. They celebrate Finnish holidays, have skiing competitions, and hold festivals. They organize a yearly Finnfest to celebrate their rich culture. To mark the beginning of the new millennium, Finns in America and Canada celebrated together at the FinnGrandFest 2000 in Toronto.

MINI FINLAND

The Salolampi Language Village has authentic Finnish lodges and cabins in the midst of forests near Bemidji, Minnesota, on Turtle River Lake. The school's curriculum focuses on immersion education in Finnish culture and language. In summer, the participants are mainly children and teenagers, but in spring and autumn, adults also take courses.

On March 16, Finns in North America celebrate Saint Urho Day. This day honors a fictional saint of Finnish-Americans. Saint Urho supposedly fought grasshoppers with a fork and saved Finnish wine production in America!

Well-Known in America

Several Finnish-Americans have become famous. John Morton signed the Declaration of Independence in 1776. Filmmaker Renny Harlin has achieved much success in Hollywood. Esa-Pekka Salonen is conductor of the Los Angeles Philharmonic Orchestra and one of the top conductors in the world.

Composer Jean Sibelius is the most famous name in Finnish music, but others are known internationally as well. The Finnish band Värttinä has captured the heart of Americans with its unique brand of music originating from Finnish folk songs. Finnish musician Maria Kalaniemi is one of the world's most talented accordionists, and soprano Karita Mattila sang a work by Sibelius at the multinational millennium New Year concert.

Below: **Rock festivals in Finland are sold out as often as those in the United States. The Finnish band Värttinä is also popular with Americans.**

Above: **Young Finns enjoy American television, MTV, and fast food.**

Finnish Clubs

In addition to Finnfests in both the United States and Canada, Finns in North America have many organizations that promote Finnish culture and boost relations between the countries. The Finlandia Foundation organizes Finnish-American cultural exchanges and supports other Finnish organizations in their efforts to preserve and promote Finnish culture.

The Finlanders at the University of Minnesota is a student organization for people interested in anything Finnish. Founded in 1992, its members are Finns, Americans, and international students who are interested in the Finnish language, culture, and lifestyle. They organize short trips, get-togethers, and sauna sessions. They also started the Nordic Roots Festival.

Kipinä-Kerho in Washington, D.C. has been promoting Finland and the Finnish language for over fifty years. Today, the group publishes a newsletter covering important Finnish events in Washington and Finland.

American Culture in Finland

Finland is sometimes known as the most Americanized country in Europe. U.S. movies, music, and culture have invaded Finnish homes, and other signs of America exist all over Finland. McDonald's restaurants and Timex watches, the best selling watches in North America, are everywhere. The American Bookshop is the largest English-language bookstore in Finland, carrying more than 15,000 titles. Like Americans, Finns have enormous supermarkets in sprawling suburban malls.

Finns are also avid American soap opera fans. They tend to speak American English, which they pick up from movies and television shows. They enjoy American MTV and wear American baseball caps, T-shirts, and baggy jeans.

There are only about two thousand Americans living in Finland, and most of them are employed by American or Finnish companies. To protect its own workforce, Finland has a closed-door policy regarding foreign labor, which means it will only employ foreigners in jobs that cannot be filled by locals.

Below: **The Kiasma Museum of Contemporary Art in Helsinki was designed by American architect Steven Holl.**

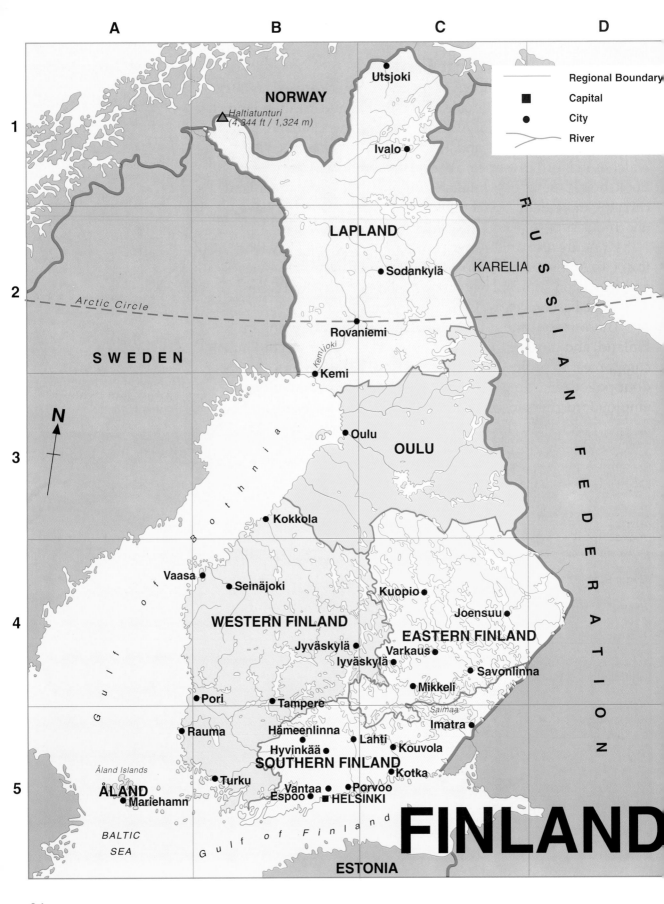

	A	B	C	D

NORWAY

Utsjoki

▲ Haltiatunturi
(4,344 ft / 1,324 m)

Ivalo

LAPLAND

● Sodankylä

KARELIA

Arctic Circle

S W E D E N

Rovaniemi

Kemijoki

● Kemi

N

● Oulu

OULU

● Kokkola

Vaasa ●

● Seinäjoki

Kuopio ●

Joensuu ●

WESTERN FINLAND

EASTERN FINLAND

Jyväskylä ●

Varkaus ●

Iyväskylä ●

Savonlinna ●

Mikkeli ●

● Pori

Saimaa

● Tampere

Imatra ●

● Rauma

Hämeenlinna ●

● Lahti

Kouvola ●

Hyvinkää ●

SOUTHERN FINLAND

Kotka ●

Åland Islands

● Turku

Vantaa ●

Porvoo ●

ÅLAND

Espoo ● ■ HELSINKI

● Mariehamn

**BALTIC
SEA**

Gulf of Finland

FINLAND

ESTONIA

Legend:
— Regional Boundary
■ Capital
● City
~ River

Above: Boats and ships in all shapes and sizes ply the thousands of lakes and many rivers of Finland.

Åland A5
Åland Islands A5
Arctic Circle A2–D2

Baltic Sea A5

Eastern Finland C4–D4
Espoo B5
Estonia B5-C5

Gulf of Bothnia A5–B3
Gulf of Finland B5–C5

Haltiatunturi B1
Hämeenlinna B5
Helsinki B5
Hyvinkää B5

Imatra C5
Ivalo C1
Iyväskylä C4

Joensuu C4
Jyväskylä B4

Karelia C2
Kemi B3
Kemijoki River B2
Kokkola B3
Kotka C5
Kouvola C5
Kuopio C4

Lahti B5
Lapland B1–C3

Mariehamn A5
Mikkeli C4

Norway A2–C1

Oulu (city) B3
Oulu (province) B3–C3

Pori B4
Porvoo B5

Rauma A5
Rovaniemi B2
Russian Federation
    C1–D5

Saimaa Lake C5
Savonlinna C4
Seinäjoki B4
Sodankylä C2
Southern Finland B5–C5
Sweden A4–B2

Tampere B4

Turku B5

Utsjoki C1

Vaasa B4
Vantaa B5
Varkaus C4

Western Finland B4–B5

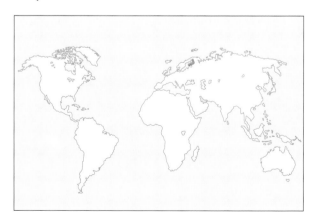

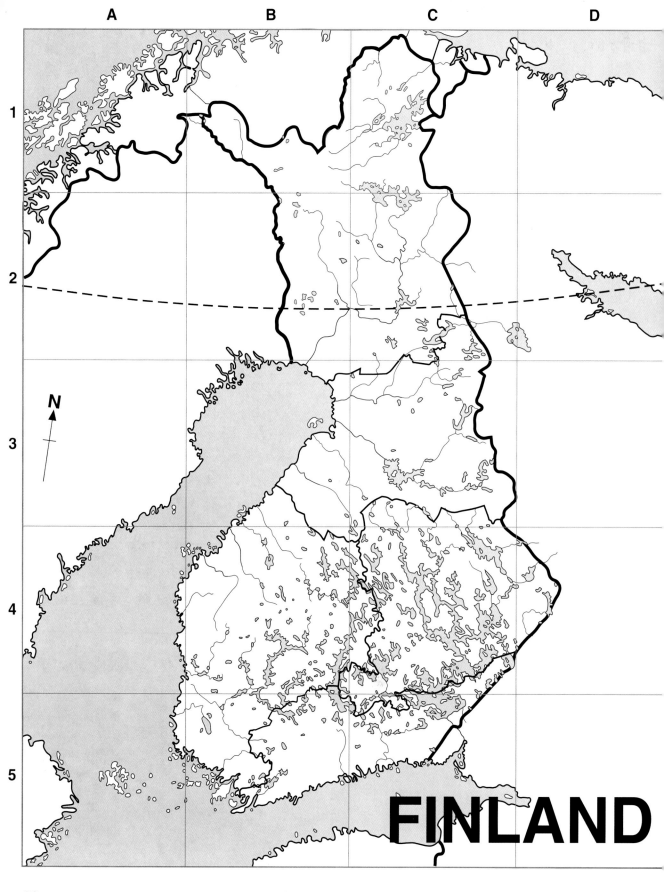

FINLAND

How Is Your Geography?

Learning to identify the main geographical areas and points of a country can be challenging. Although it may seem difficult at first to memorize the locations and spellings of major cities or the names of mountain ranges, rivers, deserts, lakes, and other prominent physical features, the end result of this effort can be very rewarding. Places you previously did not know existed will suddenly come to life when referred to in world news, whether in newspapers, television reports, or other books and reference sources. This knowledge will make you feel a bit closer to the rest of the world, with its fascinating variety of cultures and physical geography.

Used in a classroom setting, the instructor can make duplicates of this map using a copy machine. (PLEASE DO NOT WRITE IN THIS BOOK!) Students can then fill in any requested information on their individual map copies. Used one-on-one, the student can also make copies of the map on a copy machine and use them as a study tool. The student can practice identifying place names and geographical features on his or her own.

Above: **Reindeer are raised in Finland for their meat and as tourist attractions at Santa's Village.**

Finland at a Glance

Official Name	Republic of Finland (Suomen Tasavalta)
Capital	Helsinki
Official Languages	Finnish (93.5 percent), Swedish (6.3 percent)
Population	5,158,000 (1999 estimate)
Land Area	130,128 square miles (337,032 square km)
Provinces	Åland, Eastern Finland, Lapland, Oulu, Southern Finland, Western Finland
Highest Point	Haltiatunturi 4,344 feet (1,324 m)
Ethnic Groups	Finnish, Romany, Sami, Swedish
Literacy Rate	100 percent
Major Religions	Eastern Orthodox, Evangelical Lutheran
Important Festivals	Christmas, Easter, Independence Day, Midsummer, Mother's Day, Vappu (May Day)
Natural Resources	Copper, iron ore, silver, timber, zinc
Major Exports	Chemicals, electronics, furniture, machinery, metal, paper, ships, textiles, timber
Major Imports	Consumer goods, mineral fuels, raw materials
Flag	Blue Nordic cross on white background
Imperial Crest	Finnish lion bearing a sword and stepping on a curved sword, surrounded by nine roses
National Anthem	Maamme Laulu (Our Land)
Currency	markka (FIM 6.6115 = U.S. $1 as of 2000)

Opposite: **Post-World War II buildings in Helsinki are distinctly Finnish — traditional, somewhat ornate styles designed to blend in with their surroundings.**

Glossary

Finnish Vocabulary

glogi (GLUR-gee): a sweet drink made with cinnamon, ginger, raisins, and almonds and served hot.

Juhannus (yu-HAH-nohs): Midsummer holiday.

Kaamos (KAH-mohs): a time of year in Finland when the sun does not rise.

kalakukko (KAH-lah-koo-koh): rye bread wrapped around fish and bacon.

Kalevala (KAH-le-vah-lah): Finland's national epic.

karjalanpaisti (KAR-ee-LARN-pah-ih-ees-tee): meat casserole.

kota (KOH-tah): a Sami tent.

lohikeitto (LOH-ih-KAY-ee-toh): salmon soup.

pesäpallo (pay-SAH-PARL-loh): a variation of American baseball.

piparkakku (pee-PAHR-kah-koo): ginger cookies, usually eaten during Christmas.

pulla (POO-lah): sweet bread with cardamom, sprinkled with sugar.

rapu (RAH-poo): crayfish.

sisu (SEE-soo): strength and determination to persevere.

Suomi (SOR-mee): Finland.

Vappu (VAH-poo): May Day.

English Vocabulary

adversity: a time of difficulties or problems.

affiliate: associate.

angling: fishing with a hook and line.

arable: fit for crop production.

archipelago: a group of islands.

autonomous: independent.

avid: eager.

barbaric: rough and uncivilized.

biodegradable: able to be broken down into simpler particles.

comprehensive school: a school that offers a complete course of study.

conglomerate: a big company made up of smaller companies.

congregation: a crowd or assembly of people, often in a church.

coniferous: cone-bearing, such as a pine or fir tree.

conservative: traditional, unprogressive.

constitution: a set of laws that describes the powers and duties of the government.

defiance: the act of refusing to obey authority.

deforestation: the large-scale cutting down of trees.

developing nation: a country that is in the process of acquiring industrial technology.

emigrate: to move away from a country.

enlightened: well-informed and progressive.

epic: a work of prose or poetry that describes extraordinary events and often the history of a nation.

ethnic pride: pride in race and culture.

fauna: animal life.

fell: chop down.

feminist: person who believes that women should have the same rights and opportunities as men.

flora: plant life.

fly fishing: angling or fishing with artificial bait tied to a hook.

functional: designed to be useful.

gourmet: a person who enjoys eating high-quality food.

immersion education: a method of learning that concentrates deeply on a specific discipline or area of study.

immigrant: a person who moves to a country to make a home there.

industrialize: to develop factories and businesses on a large scale.

infrastructure: underlying foundation or basic framework.

latitude: the degree of distance from the equator moving north or south.

medieval: relating to or dating from between the eleventh and fifteenth centuries.

metallurgy: the science and technology of extracting and refining metals.

migration: the act of moving from one country or region to another.

modernism: the ideas and methods of modern art.

municipal: relating to local government matters.

municipality: an urban government unit.

neutral: impartial, uninvolved.

nomads: people who move from place to place.

Nordic: describing a person, object, or place from northern Europe.

ombudsman: an impartial public official who investigates complaints by private citizens against government agencies or officials.

organic architecture: a building style that uses characteristics or features of living organisms.

pagan: worshiper of many gods.

parish: an area served by a particular church; also, the people living in that area.

parliament: council or legislative assembly of a government.

pastoral: relating to the countryside.

polytechnic: a school that concentrates on technical arts and applied sciences.

pulp: substance made from wood fibers and used in making paper.

realm: kingdom.

reparation: payment for damage.

republic: representative government.

revenue: the total earnings produced by a specific source.

Romany: a people better known as Gypsies. Found in many European countries, they are believed to have migrated from Asia.

sauna: a hot steam bath; a room or building that contains a sauna.

segregate: to keep two groups of people or objects physically apart from each other.

sparse: meager.

taboo: forbidden.

taciturn: reluctant to converse.

technology: the use of scientific knowledge in industry.

teepee: a round, pointed tent.

telecommunications: communications at a distance, as by telephone or Internet.

terrain: ground.

toxic: poisonous.

urban: characteristic of a city.

More Books to Read

Children of All Lands: Little Lauri of Finland. Bernadine Bailey (Booksmith-USA)

The Enchanted Wood and Other Tales from Finland. World Folklore series. Norma J. Livo, George O. Livo, Lauren J. Livo, and Steve Wilcox (Libraries Unlimited)

Finland. Cultures of the World series. Tan Chung Lee (Benchmark)

Finland. Enchantment of the World series. Sylvia McNair (Children's Press)

Finland. Festivals of the World series. Chung Lee Tan (Gareth Stevens)

Finland. Major World Nations series. Alan James (Chelsea House)

Finland in Pictures. Visual Geography series. David A. Boehm (Lerner)

The Grandchildren of the Vikings. World's Children series. Reijo Harkonen and Matti A. Pitkanen (Carolrhoda Books)

The Magic Storysinger: From the Finnish Epic Kalevala. M. E. A. McNeil (Stemmer House Publishers, Inc.)

The Maiden of Northland: A Hero Tale of Finland. Aaron Shepard and Carol Schwartz (Atheneum)

A Short History of Finland. Fred Singleton and Anthony F. Upton (Cambridge University Press)

Videos

Video Visits — Finland, Fresh and Original. (IVN Entertainment)

Wild Arctic. (WGBH Boston Video)

Web Sites

www.finland.org

www.itv.se/boreale/samieng.htm

virtual.finland.fi

Due to the dynamic nature of the Internet, some web sites stay current longer than others. To find additional web sites, use a reliable search engine with one or more of the following keywords to help you locate information about Finland. Keywords: *Helsinki*, Kalevala, *Lapland, midnight sun, Nokia, reindeer, Sami, Santa Claus, sauna, Scandinavia.*

Index

Aalto, Alvar 31, 45, 60, 61
Aaltonen, Wäino 31
Adventists 26
Africa 72, 77, 78
Agricola, Mikael 26, 28, 29
agriculture 6, 9, 18, 63, 80
Ahtisaari, Martti 75
Åland Islands 6, 8
All Saints Ice Regatta 53
American Bookshop 85
animals 9, 37, 62, 63, 64, 65, 66, 67
architecture 31, 44, 45
Arctic Academy 55
Arctic Circle 7, 8, 69
aurora borealis
    (*see* northern lights)

bonfires 38, 58, 59
Bosnia 14, 72, 77
brown bears 9, 65

California 79, 80
Canada 75, 76, 79, 82
Canth, Minna 15, 33, 73
Catholicism 26
Christianity 11, 26, 38, 39, 58
Christmas 39, 68, 69, 71
Clinton, Bill 75, 77
coffee 37, 41
Cold War 76
computers 47
Conference on Security and
    Cooperation in Europe
    (CSCE) 14, 76
crayfish 40, 41, 71

dance 33
Declaration of
    Independence (U.S.) 83
deforestation 64

design 18, 60, 61, 65
Donner, Jorn 33

Easter 38
Eastern Orthodox Church 10, 26, 27
economy 14, 18, 19, 62, 63
education 24, 25, 32
elks 9, 34
English language 24, 29, 85
environmental issues 34, 43, 64, 65
Equality Act 72
etiquette 48, 49
European Union 14, 78

Finland, Minnesota 80
Finlanders 84
Finlandia Foundation 84
Finlandia Hall 14, 45
Finlandia Race 36
Finnfest 82
Finnish American Chamber of
    Commerce 77
Finnish Environment
    Protection Association 64
Finnish Evangelical Lutheran
    Church 81
Finnish language 24, 26, 28, 29, 82, 84
Finnish National Ballet 33
Finnish National Museum 57
Finnish Socialist
    Federation 81
Finnish Workers Society 81
Finno-Ugric 10, 28, 66
fish 5, 35, 40, 41, 52, 53, 70, 71
flag 5
Ford, Gerald 77
forestry 7, 9, 62, 63, 64, 65
Forestry Act 64

Gallen-Kallela, Akseli 31
German language 24, 28
Germany 13, 19, 75, 78
Giscard d'Estaing, Valéry 77
government 16, 17
Greece 68
Gulf of Bothnia 6
Gulf of Finland 6, 11
Gustave III 11

Häkkinen, Mika 37
Halonen, Tarja 16, 23, 73
Haltiatunturi 7
Häme Castle 56, 57
Häme peoples 10
Hämeenlinna 57
Harlin, Renny 33, 82, 83
Helsinki 11, 14, 17, 21, 24, 30, 31, 33, 39, 45, 57, 75, 76, 85
Helsinki Summit 1997 75
Holl, Steven 85

immigrants 79, 80, 81, 82
independence 5, 12, 30, 39
infant mortality 22
Internet 13, 47

Jehovah's Witnesses 26
Jews 26
Jotuni, Maria 33

Kaamos 8, 54
Kalaniemi, Maria 83
Kalevala 15, 29, 30, 31, 61
Karelia 10, 11, 13
Kekkonen, Urho 14, 77
Kipinä-Kerho 84
Kiasma Museum of
    Contemporary Art 85
Kirvesniemi, Marja-Liisa 36
Kirvesniemi, Harri 36
Kivi, Alexis 29, 33

Kone 19, 78
kota 67
Kuopio Dance and Music Festival 33
Kurri, Jari 36

Laine, Edvin 33
Lapland 7, 11, 20, 54, 55, 64, 66
Lebanon 14
Linna, Väinö 29, 33
Lipponen, Paavo 16, 78
Litmanen, Jari 35
Lönnrot, Elias 15, 29
Lutheranism 26, 27, 81

Mäkinen, Tommi 37
Mannerheim, Carl Gustaf Emil 12, 15
Marshall Plan 77
Massachusetts 75, 79
Matikainen, Marjo 36
Mattila, Karita 73, 83
May Day 38
Michigan 75, 79, 80, 81
midnight sun 6, 8, 54
Midsummer 38, 58, 59, 82
Minnesota 75, 79, 80, 82, 84
mobile telephones 13, 46, 47, 49
Mollberg, Rauni 33
Morton, John 83
movies 33
music 32, 33, 83

name days 27
New Sweden 79
New York 79, 80
Nicholas, Bishop 68
Nokia 19, 47, 78
North Atlantic Treaty Organization (NATO) 76
northern lights 6, 43, 54, 55
Nurmi, Paavo 15, 31, 35
Nuutajarvi Glassworks 60
Nykänen, Matti 36

Nylund, Felix 30

Olympics 15, 31, 35, 36
Oregon 79, 80
Organization for Economic Cooperation and Development (OECD) 76

Paasikivi-Kekkonen line 14
Pacius, Fredrik 32
pesäpallo 35
Porvoo 17
provinces 17

reindeer 37, 41, 42, 43, 63, 66, 67, 69
Ritola, Ville 35
rock festivals 32, 83
Romany 20
Rovaniemi 53, 69
Russia 5, 10, 11, 12, 13, 14, 17, 19, 30, 75, 78, 79
Russian language 24

Saariaho, Kaija 73
Saimaa Lake 7
Saint Urho Day 83
salmon 9, 40, 53, 70
Salolampi Language Village 82
Salonen, Esa-Pekka 32, 83
Sami 11, 20, 66, 67, 69
Santa Claus 39, 43, 68, 69
Santa Claus Village 69
sauna 20, 43, 50, 51, 59, 82
Savonlinna 57, 74, 75
Savonlinna Opera Festival 57
Savoy vase 60, 61
Schmidt, Helmut 77
Selänne, Teemu 36
Sibelius, Jean 31, 32, 83
Sillanpää, Frans Eemil 29
sisu 21, 82
Social Democratic Party 16, 73
Sodankylä 55

Soviet Union 13, 14, 15, 76
sports 35, 36, 37, 52, 53
Stone Age 10
Strategic Arms Limitation Talks (SALT) 14, 76
Sulkava Rowing Regatta 53
Suomalainen, Timo 45
Suomalainen, Tuomo 45
Swedish language 24, 28

Tampere 18, 21, 26
Telecom Finland 47
Temppeliaukio Church 44, 45
theater 33
Treaty of Friendship, Cooperation, and Mutual Assistance 13, 76
Treaty of Nöteborg 11
Turku 10, 21, 26, 33, 55, 57
Turku Castle 10, 31, 57
Turku Cathedral 55

United Kingdom 19, 78
United Nations 14, 72, 76, 77
United States 14, 19, 75, 76, 77, 78, 79, 80
Unknown Soldier 29, 33
Uotinen, Jorma 33
Uspenski Cathedral 27

Värttinä 83
Vatanen, Ari 37

Washington (state) 79, 80
Washington, D.C. 84
welfare 17, 73
Wilderness Act 64
Wilson, Harold 77
Winter War 12, 13, 15
Wisconsin 80
witches 38
women 15, 23, 72, 73
World War II 12, 13, 29, 77, 79

Yeltsin, Boris 75